CRUSAD

CW0060946

'I'm about to launch a crusade, Sister Bergman, and I'm counting on you to become a fellow crusader.' With a whole hospital full of people only too willing to help him get the money he needed for a laser machine, why did the new consultant surgeon, Sebastian Carr, have to pick on *her*, Valda Bergman wondered . . .

Helen Upshall lives in Bournemouth with her husband, now retired. When quite young she became interested in Doctor Nurse stories, reading her much older sister's magazine serials instead of getting on with the dusting, so it was a natural progression to go into nursing in the late 1940s. Since she took up writing, ideas have come from a variety of sources—personal experiences of relatives and friends, and documentaries on television. *Crusading Consultant* is Helen Upshall's ninth Doctor Nurse Romance.

CRUSADING CONSULTANT

BY

HELEN UPSHALL

MILLS & BOON LIMITED
15-16 BROOK'S MEWS
LONDON W1A 1DR

First published in Great Britain 1987 by Mills & Boon Limited

© Helen Upshall 1987

Australian copyright 1987 Philippine copyright 1987 This edition 1987

ISBN 0 263 75762 5

Set in Monotype Times 10 on 10.5 pt. 03-0687-57594

Typeset in Great Britain by Associated Publishing Services Printed and bound in Great Britain by William Collins

For Nora and Carlos,
with love

CHAPTER ONE

SISTER Valda Bergman placed two fingers on her lips and as she watched the lift doors slide noiselessly together she raised the same two fingers in an affectionate parting wave to the man inside the lift.

Now he was gone, and she remained staring at the closed doors in pensive reflection. Then her attention was drawn to the light above which illuminated the numbered button as the lift descended, 3, 2, 1, G—Adrian had reached street level and she visualised the tall, suave figure of the special man in her life striding away, oblivious of the admiring glances his proud bearing, thick black wavy hair and dark eyes evoked.

The light on the adjoining lift flashed from 1 to 2; someone else was on the way up, or was it Adrian returning for yet another farewell kiss? Then running footsteps could be heard on the stone stairs and before Valda could return to her office an unfamiliar figure reached the landing with lithesome ease.

'I'm afraid visiting time is over for today,' Valda said, believing him to be a patient's relative.

Amber-coloured eyes flashed momentary annoyance, then, with a slight incline of his head, he muttered darkly: 'Really?'

Valda was still mildly euphoric from Adrian's surprise visit, but gradually she managed to set her mind on a collision course with the arrogant man who made no attempt to hide his contempt for a mere hospital Sister. His glance idled over her figure-flattering uniform.

'I'm looking for Sister Bergman's office, preferably with Sister Bergman in it,' he said. His tone was a touch too autocratic, his manner of speech almost too perfect, and yet there was the hint of a dual personality hidden beneath the exterior arrogance.

'You're looking for me?' Valda raised her eyebrows at the fact that this stranger knew her name. 'Ah, you must be Mrs Kepple's husband—no—she's *Miss* Kepple,' Valda remembered, slightly bemused.

'I'd better introduce myself, Sister. Sebastian Carr.'

Valda felt the blood drain from her face as he held out his hand. She hadn't expected his handshake to be limp, but she wasn't prepared for the uncompromising iron clasp which rendered her fingers useless for several seconds even after he had released them. She knew him by name only—a name which wasn't difficult to remember, and which had conjured up an image of a bespectacled, pompous little man. Sebastian Carr in the flesh wasn't quite what she had expected.

'How do you do, sir,' Valda managed politely, her cheeks now pinker than usual. 'I wasn't expecting you to arrive at this end of the day.'

'Does it matter?'

'No . . . no, of course not.' She led the way across the stone-floored landing, her tread light, a mere whisper of noise, whereas his was firm with a decisive rhythm in her wake. She had just told a bare-faced lie; of course it mattered having a consultant visit a ward when the Sister-in-charge had only half an hour to complete her report before the night staff took over. But the new consultant was hardly likely to make allowances for the fact that the Sister-in-charge had just entertained her boy-friend for twenty minutes during working hours. Well—Dr Adrian Wallace had visited a patient of his . . . They walked silently past the pay-telephones and various cupboards to an airy room where the window was wide open to allow the fresh summer breeze to float across to Valda as she pushed open the door. She walked to her desk, aware of the newcomer's smouldering gaze on her back. She decided against sitting down, but when the new ophthalmic surgeon sat in her visitor's chair she assumed she was expected to take up her formal position behind the desk.

'It's a bit late to show you round, Mr Carr,' she began.

'There's plenty of time to do that, Sister.' He leaned back in the chair in a relaxed position, crossing his legs, and from the gold chain looped across his immaculate waistcoat he pulled out a gold watch, read the time, and with a smile put it away.

'I expected to find you busy writing your report before you go off duty.'

'I . . . I have that to finish,' she explained, feeling awkward as a flush spread across her face. 'One of the local GPs called in to see one of his patients.' Why was she behaving in such a guilty fashion if that was the truth? And why did Sebastian Carr's presence unnerve her and his smile of amusement at her discomfort annoy her?

'I arrived here at lunchtime so I've been getting to know my team, and way about. I just thought I'd pay my respects—you are, after all, an important part of my team, you'll be caring for my in-patients.'

'We do communicate pretty well on the whole—'

'I want us to do more than just communicate, Sister Bergman,' he cut in. 'I'm about to launch a crusade and I'm counting on you to become a fellow crusader.'

'What kind of crusade?' Valda asked with wide-eyed curiosity.

'I've ordered a laser machine for Addlefield's Eye Unit,' he said confidently, 'even though I've been warned there aren't sufficient funds to pay for it, so I'm hoping the staff here will join forces with me to raise the necessary amount.'

Valda sat back in her chair, taken aback by the cheek of the man.

'You do realise how important a laser machine is in eye treatment?' he challenged.

'Yes—but the new hospital and scanner have cost so much. Local people are always being asked for money, I'm not sure they will respond to more fund-raising events.'

'Then it's up to us to see that we emphasise the importance of such equipment. Just because the new Addlefield Memorial Hospital has all the latest equipment and the old Addlefield Hospital has been designated for Ear, Nose, Throat and Eyes it doesn't mean we have to be content with out-dated methods and old-fashioned equipment.'

'It may be an old building, Mr Carr, but we are all as up-to-date as our colleagues in the splendid new building,' Valda defended.

'Good—then you agree with me that a laser machine is top priority?'

'I . . . I'm not in charge here—it isn't for me to say,' she hedged.

'I have it on the best authority that you're one of Addlefield's most competent nursing sisters.'

She lowered her gaze in embarrassment, then realising that he was merely flattering her to get her on his side she flashed him an angry frown.

'There's no room here for incompetent staff,' she retorted.

'Then we shouldn't have much difficulty in finding plenty of support in our efforts to raise money for the machine.' He stood up and gripped the back of the chair with even more force than he had used to paralyse her fingers earlier. 'I'll leave you to think about it, Sister,' he added, with a guarded threatening tone. 'Perhaps you can use your persuasive charms on all your staff—we'll have another chat soon about how we'll raise funds.' He strode away, and she listened to the purposeful tread until it faltered and she realised that he couldn't find his way back to the stairs. She was about to go to his aid when she heard voices. The night staff were arriving so one of them could point him in the right direction, she decided.

Valda tried to get back into the spirit of her report. First Adrian had interrupted her, but now thoughts of him were filmed by the influence of the new consultant. He was handsome, though not as handsome as her Adrian, she gloated. This Mr Carr was older, and in spite of his well-cut grey suit and silver-grey tie with pink chevrons to match his pink shirt, there was something tough about his attitude. She couldn't really visualise him climbing a mountain, but she felt that physical exercise of some sort stimulated him. She managed a sly smile to herself, guessing what kind of physical exercise would be attributed to Mr Sebastian Carr by the rest of Addlefield's staff! Any newcomer, however insignificant, had to be held to the light for appraisal. He would be watched, and studied both as a man and surgeon. The staff loved a good gossip just as they loved someone new to gossip about, and Valda felt a moment's pity for Sebastian Carr. With a name like that didn't he need everyone's pity she thought with a wry smile.

'Hi, Val,' Pam Gardner, night Sister, greeted. 'Not ready for me yet?'

Valda sighed. 'Adrian came in to see Mrs Roache, and then the new consultant visited me—you've probably just met him.'

'The man I've just shown the way out?'

Valda nodded. 'He refused the lift,' Pam went on. 'Is he some kind of nut?'

Valda grinned. 'Probably, with a name like Sebastian Carr!'

'Mm—rather superior—and he's quite a dish, I thought. What do we know about him?'

'Only that he's one for crusades. He hasn't even started work here yet and already he's ordered a laser machine.'

'Gosh, that's marvellous. I've been reading about them—what every good eye hospital should have.'

'But not when you're an old hospital only tolerated because you can make use of an obsolete building. The new Addlefield Memorial is the one to sport the latest in techniques and machinery.'

'Don't be so defeatist, Val,' Pam chided. 'We ought to push for better equipment.'

'Only to be slapped down still further with cutbacks.'

'And that's all false economy. If people need treatment it's cheaper in the long run to give them the best at the beginning.'

'Try telling that to the powers-that-be.' Valda went on working on her report.

'He must have had the go-ahead from the hospital board to order the laser machine.'

'Mm—but we have to pay for it.'

'What do you mean—*we*?'

'He's going to organise fund-raising,' Val said. 'Poor Addlefield—the people are always being asked to support some project or other.'

'It's amazing where the money comes from with so much unemployment everywhere.'

'You can't get blood out of a stone,' Valda retorted. 'People can only give so much.'

'Not like you to be so negative, Val. Sounds as if the noble Sebastian Carr has got on the wrong side of you.'

'He's made me late,' she grumbled, then with a prominent stab of her pen she lifted her tired shoulders and stretched.

'Were you—*are* you in a hurry?' Pam asked.

'No—but we've a fair list for surgery tomorrow.'

'Don't worry—we'll see that they're ready.' Pam took her place beside Valda at the long desk as Valda started her report with details of a new admission.

'Miss Kepple's come in as an emergency detachment. Theatre tomorrow,' Valda explained. 'She's over sixty, never been in hospital before so is terrified and needs lots of reassurance. She seems to be equally—perhaps more—concerned for her dog than herself. She drove herself in from her GP's surgery so the police are going to take the car back to her home for her. Ray Pyke didn't dare let her go home as she begged to be allowed to do or she'd have never returned. He can't be too sure that he can save her sight as it is. She had her dog with her apparently, so the police are dropping him off at the kennels. Poor soul, she's rather distressed, and I don't imagine she'll give you much peace tonight.'

After further discussion about some of the thirty-two patients in the Eye Unit, Valda left the wards and took the lift down to the ground floor where she let herself out of the side door and walked across the garden to Conifer Lodge, the Sisters' Home. It was a fine old Victorian house, now modernised into bed-sits for nursing Sisters who were unable to find accommodation elsewhere. Many of them were middle-aged—younger girls usually stayed at Conifer Lodge only until they found a flat to rent or could afford to buy their own homes. Valda stayed for convenience to be near her work; when weekends off came round she drove home to the picturesque village of Deasley, eight miles out of Addlefield, nestling in a valley in the Cotswold Hills, where her father, a retired police sergeant, lived alone. One day she had visions of sharing a nice new home with Adrian—that's if he ever proposed. She counted herself lucky, and was flattered that after visiting her father, Howard Bergman, when he'd suffered a mild heart attack, Adrian had shown increasing interest in her until now she reckoned they were going steady.

She showered and washed her hair, and was thankful to slip beneath the light duvet where she could dream about her extremely handsome boy-friend.

Valda went on duty early next morning as it was a theatre day, and was confronted almost at once by Ray Pyke, senior registrar, and Danny Banks the duty anaesthetist for the day.

'Hi, poppet,' the latter greeted in his usual friendly style. 'Hope you're feeling on top form, today promises to be full of excitement.'

'Why, what's happened?'

'Miss Kepple—new admission overnight,' Danny explained.

'She came in just before I went off duty,' Valda informed him.

'Then you know she's a difficult one.'

'Not difficult, Doctor, just scared to death and insecure,' Valda said.

'So *you* calm her down,' Danny retorted. 'I checked her over last night and thought I'd convinced her that she was in capable hands, but, ye Gods, is she suspicious!'

'Of what? You?' Valda grinned impishly. 'Can't blame her, can you?'

'All right, Miss Smarty-Pants, cut out the personal quips and be serious. I don't envy you having to administer her pre-med—we're all going to need danger money.'

'Stop exaggerating, Danny, no one's that bad.'

'Miss Kepple is—and of all the days to have such a one.'

'What's special about today?'

'Haven't you heard? Our new consultant is coming to take over today.'

'I thought he did that yesterday,' Valda retorted cryptically.

Danny eyed her suspiciously as he perched on the corner of her desk. Valda folded up her long sleeves and put on her white sleeve-bands.

'Oh yes?' he queried sarcastically, waiting for further information.

'He called here before I went off duty,' Valda hastily explained.

'To see Miss Kepple?'

Valda shook her head. 'No—he's about to launch a

money-making campaign to pay for the laser machine
he's ordered and we're all expected to support him.'

Danny played with the pens in Valda's pen-tray as
he thought this over. 'Is that right?' he commented
slowly, then he lifted Valda's face by placing one finger
beneath her chin. 'Seems he knew exactly who to
approach first.'

Valda tossed her head so that Danny's finger fell
away from her chin. 'You've got an evil mind,' she
accused him. 'Someone just happened to mention that
Sister Bergman was in charge of Eye Wards so he came
looking for me. I've yet to find out who pointed him in
my direction, though I can only think it must have been
Matron. I was just seeing Adrian off.'

'No wonder you're blushing—with shame,' Danny
reproached, standing up and waving a condemning
finger at her. 'Don't let it happen again, Sister,' he said
in a mocking voice. 'You aren't allowed to entertain
boy-friends either on the wards or in your room.'

'Corridors and lifts aren't mentioned though,' Valda
responded with a facetious chuckle.

'Poppet, just lead me to the lift!'

'I'd better lead you to Miss Kepple, I think.'

Danny groaned. 'Don't remind me.'

'Cheer up, we'll see that she's calm by the time you
get her. Where's she placed on the list?'

They consulted the list on the desk.

'Mm,' Valda mused. 'Last, because she was a late
admission I suppose. What say we move her to the first
one after the lunch break?'

'That should give you time to charm her with your
magic spell,' Danny said ruefully.

'A little gentle persuasion, Danny; reassurance is all
she needs,' Valda said confidently.

'It's me who needs the reassurance. I'll leave you to
it. I must be ready for his "Nibs".'

Danny took himself off, but returned almost at once
following Sebastian Carr.

'I believe you've met Sister Bergman?' Danny was saying as they walked up to her desk.

'I have indeed. Good morning, Sister. Let's see what we can do to help Miss Kepple.' Sebastian started for the door and Valda followed, remembering to pick up Miss Kepple's notes from the desk.

'Mr Pyke, the senior registrar, saw her last evening,' Valda began by way of putting him in the picture, but he hurried out into the corridor and with a curt wave of his hand indicated that he wished to be shown to the small room where Pam Gardner was with Miss Kepple.

'Hallo, Miss Kepple. How do you feel this morning? Full of apprehension I expect? My name is Carr and I shall be in the theatre to see what we can do to save your sight later on today,' he introduced swiftly but kindly.

Miss Kepple, pale and with a look of terror, clutched at Sebastian's arm. 'Doctor, please, I must go home. I shouldn't have come—it's all a mistake. I can see all right, I can see you clearly,' she insisted. 'I must get my Carlos out of those dreadful kennels.'

Sebastian Carr did the unconventional thing and sat on the side of the bed. He cupped one hand over her right eye. 'What colour eyes do I have, Miss Kepple?' he asked.

There was no immediate answer and rather than put any strain on the left eye he took his hand away and picked up the patient's trembling fingers in his.

'You aren't helping yourself, my dear,' he consoled gently. 'You know you have almost no sight now because the retina has become detached. We want to try to put it right if we can. All these nice people are here to look after you. Within a few hours the worst part will be over.'

'But I'm terrified,' Miss Kepple admitted, her voice breaking.

'We understand. Any new experience is frightening,' Sebastian agreed.

'You won't put me to sleep will you?' she begged.

Sebastian smiled and patted her head. 'Try to be sensible, Miss Kepple. You know we have to or we couldn't possibly do anything to help you.'

'I'll never wake up,' she sobbed, 'I know I won't.'

'You don't think that when you go to bed at night now do you?' he asked with a smile.

'Sometimes,' she whispered after a pause.

'We're going to see that you do wake up,' he promised. 'And if you do all that we ask you'll be going home in less than a week.'

'A week,' Miss Kepple moaned. 'A whole week for poor Carlos in that awful place.'

'We'll talk about Carlos later,' Sebastian assured her, and after more comforting words he finally left her.

'We'll get on,' he said to Danny briskly, then with a brief glance towards Valda, said: 'Keep an eye, Sister. I know you have other patients, but she does need special care. If you can't spare the time yourself, give her your most caring nurse.'

Valda and Pam went back to the office.

'He cares,' Pam said as if she had expected him not to.

'We all should,' Valda said tersely, 'or we oughtn't to be in this job.'

'Doesn't go with his image,' Pam said sarcastically. 'Just shows, you can't go by appearances. Handsome men don't usually have much depth.' She clapped her hand over her mouth. 'Sorry, Valda, Adrian's the exception of course.'

Valda smiled. She doubted that any man could come up to Adrian's perfect good looks, but she had to admit that Sebastian Carr's kindness to Miss Kepple had impressed her very much. He was almost too good to be true. Was it a case of a new broom? she wondered. He showed total dedication, and his manner had certainly gone a long way to calm Miss Kepple who wasn't afraid to voice her fears.

'I've prided myself on keeping fit,' she confided to Valda later in the morning. 'I hoped I'd never need surgery.'

'Most of us hope that, Miss Kepple.'

'You hear such rumours about things going wrong,' the patient bemoaned.

'Because people thrive on sensationalising the bad side—the good in the world is seldom proclaimed,' Valda told her.

'I suppose you're right and it's not that I'm not grateful, it's just that I never expected to be kept in. Most people have to wait ages for a bed. If only I could have gone home and made arrangements for Carlos, as well as cancelled the papers—and everything.'

Valda sat down on the chair beside Miss Kepple's bed, very aware of the patient's distress.

'What sort of dog is Carlos?' she asked kindly.

'A King Charles spaniel. I had him from a few months old. Someone threw him out of a car late one night. I live in a very tiny village, Sister, there's no more than half a dozen cottages there, so car tyres screeching round the corner woke me. I got out of bed, but the car tore off at high speed and I couldn't see anything. Next day I was walking in the garden and this little dog stood in my path. He was thin and scraggy but looked ferocious baring his teeth and snarling, so I backed all the way down to my cottage.'

'Did he attack you?' Valda asked.

'No, and if he had done it would have been to defend himself.'

'Did you send for the RSPCA or someone?' Valda pursued.

Miss Kepple managed a laugh. 'Heavens, no! I didn't want anyone else interfering, and I was afraid they'd put him down. I knew I daren't go near him, but I waited and watched, and I saw him go into my old lean-to shed right at the end of the garden. I prepared some food and left it on the path, and I called him and talked but he wouldn't come out, he just growled persistently. By the end of the first week I managed to get the food and water to the corner of the shed. He'd wait until I'd gone and he'd eat everything I'd left. By the end of the second week he came out to meet me, his tail wagging, and I knew I'd won.'

'You were very brave, Miss Kepple,' Valda said, much impressed.

'I reckon I could face a lion better than having to be put to sleep,' Miss Kepple said, trying to hide her nervousness.

Valda laughed. 'Now you're exaggerating. I promise you, a slight prick in your arm and you won't know any more until it's all over.'

'I know you mean well, Sister, and I know I'm being a nuisance, and a baby—' She began to sniffle and Valda felt compassion for her.

'Let's see if we can sort a few things out,' Valda suggested brightly. 'Is there anyone living near you who could keep an eye on your home? Cancel the milk and the papers, things like that?'

'Night Sister did all that, my dear. I know I must seem terribly ungrateful, but I'm worried mostly about Carlos. Supposing he turns on me again?'

'I'm sure they'll be kind to him, Miss Kepple, but later on when you've had your operation I'll telephone the kennels and see how he is.'

This seemed to pacify the elderly patient and when Mr Carr returned from lunch and called into the ward to see how she was, he found her drowsy from her pre-medication.

'How did you manage to calm her, Sister?' he asked Valda.

'I promised to ring the kennels to enquire after her dog. I don't know if that had anything to do with it. She's quite a courageous little lady, you know.' Valda related the story of how Miss Kepple acquired Carlos, then she laughed. 'Miss Kepple reckons she could face a lion better than be put to sleep.'

Sebastian smiled. 'It might be a good idea if you brought her along to the theatre yourself if you've gained her confidence. Have you been to lunch?' he asked.

'No, but I'll just have coffee and a bun. I want to get away on time this evening as I'm going home.'

'A rare weekend off, eh?' he enquired.

'Not a long one, just this evening and Sunday.' She almost added that she might not return until Monday morning, but that depended on Adrian. For several weeks now Adrian had been exercising his patience while Valda chose to tantalise him with whether or not she should stay with him at his flat. When she was away from Adrian she longed to see him, and knew that with the right amount of persuasion she would accept his invitation. When she was actually there though it seemed quite easy to discourage his advances. Sebastian Carr nodded politely as if indicating that her spare time was of no real interest to him, and he strode off to prepare for the rest of the day's surgery.

When the theatre bell rang Valda was already beside Miss Kepple, who smiled tremulously as she briefly opened her eyes and clutched at Valda's hand as she was moved on to the trolley and down the long corridor to the theatre which was conveniently on the same floor.

Danny Banks raised his eyebrows at Valda, half in gratitude, half in speculation, but after he had offered a few reassuring words to Miss Kepple she quickly lost consciousness, and Valda was able to leave her in the capable hands of the surgical team.

It was later, when Valda was sitting alone in an almost deserted canteen, that she pondered over her reluctance to spend the night with Adrian. The excitement of such prospects was uppermost in her mind when weekends loomed nearer, but when the time came she cooled considerably. Was she afraid of the consequences? Was it because her father in his lovable, direct way expected her to go off to live with Adrian. 'Marriage isn't sacred any more,' he frequently determined. 'Nothing is—the old values are gone.'

But Valda did have values. She wanted fun in her life, but when she pledged to love her man she wanted it to be a lasting vow, and in return expected respect—at least a ring on her finger. She gazed dismally down at her naked hands. Which would she choose, emeralds, sapphires, diamonds? Something different, she decided, even more exclusive than a pair of matching rings. She sighed, realising that Adrian had never mentioned rings, engagement or otherwise. A rubber band would be just as effective, she reflected, and that at least would be different. Insignificant though, and still looking down at her bare finger with hopeful anticipation she could only visualise a plain gold band. That would please her father, and he did like Adrian—well—she *thought* he did, even though he seldom voiced his opinion of her friends. You knew by his attitude, by what he *didn't* say, and Valda knew in her heart that it was just that which influenced her, and created that niggling doubt which suggested her father wasn't as keen on Adrian as Valda would have liked him to be. Still, she thought, it was she who would be marrying Adrian, not her father. Then she was back to square one, reminding herself that Adrian hadn't asked her to marry him—not yet. Perhaps he was waiting for confirmation of compatibility. All sorts of wild imaginings flooded her brain until common-sense prevailed. What if she weakened and gave in to Adrian only to find that their relationship was not as idyllic as they expected? She would have given in for nothing. She would be—not as pure as she wanted to be for her man. She chided herself for being thoroughly misguided and old-fashioned, and as she got up from the table she accidentally kicked the leg, making a resounding clatter on the tubular steel. It brought her up with sharp rebuke, and she returned to duty trying to dispel her contrary thoughts.

Miss Kepple was soon back in her bed, but slept peacefully on even after she had come round from the anaesthetic and Valda had stayed a while to comfort her.

The list was a long one and it became evident that any hopes Valda had of leaving early were dashed.

Adrian rang just before six o'clock, but Valda was compelled to cut short their conversation as yet another patient came back from the theatre. Valda knew she could have gone off duty at the scheduled time of four o'clock. The Superintending Sister visited Valda's ward and would have taken over, but it was Saturday, there might be casualties later, so they both appreciated the importance of seeing the day's routine carried through so that the night staff had a clear field for any eventuality.

Another hour passed before Valda felt that she could safely leave all her charges who were now back from theatre. Surgery was over for the day, the hustle and bustle reduced to normal evening quietude as some patients sat watching television and others enjoyed the privacy of their small single rooms to talk with family or friends who were visiting. All the nursing staff's attention could be focused on the ones who needed after-surgery care, and Valda finally handed over to her staff nurse before going to the locker-room and changing out of her uniform into jeans and a sweater.

As she went down the back stairs, across a patch of wild grass to an open barn-like building which served as the sisters' car-port, she wondered whether Sebastian Carr had gone home. Some surgeons made a last call to visit their patients before leaving the premises. Is that why Valda had been reluctant to go off duty? She sat in her small car and wondered why the new consultant should evoke such a feeling of curiosity.

CHAPTER TWO

WITH a swift turn of the ignition key Valda started up
the car and headed for her home village of Deasley. She
tried to concentrate on the things which might need
doing when she reached Maple Cottage, but her father
would accuse her of fussing so she knew she would have
to be diplomatic and try not to notice the dust. He
managed very well, she had to admit. He was clean,
and capable of cooking his own meals, but there were
the little extras like washing curtains which Valda liked
to do. There wouldn't be much time this weekend
though if she were to see Adrian. She sped through the
country lanes wondering whether he would be at Maple
Cottage to surprise her. It spurred her on, but when she
came to a fork in the road some two miles from Deasley
she paused, and reading the large sign which pointed in
the opposite direction to Deasley she remembered her
promise to Miss Kepple which she had not kept.

MIRANDA'S KENNELS AND CATTERY the
colourful notice advertised, and as if the car was
conscious of Valda's guilt it seemed to turn towards the
right-hand lane instead of the left. She was already late,
a few more minutes wouldn't matter. Besides, she was
curious about Miss Kepple's little dog, Carlos. She
remembered the dog she had grown up with. He had
died soon after her mother had left home. Died of a
heart attack, a broken heart they'd said, and afterwards
her father had insisted that as they were all out through
the day it wasn't fair to keep a pet.

Her car tyres crunched on the gravel drive as she
pulled into 'Miranda's', along the curving pathway to a
big patch of open space to one side of a rather spectac-

23

ular-looking bungalow. It seemed to fit 'Miranda' whoever she was, and even before Valda could get out of the car the front door opened and a tall, slim girl came out to greet her.

'Hallo, can I help?' She was around Valda's age, probably a bit younger, and she came right up to the window which Valda wound down. In the distance dogs could be heard barking and from the back of the bungalow two red setters appeared, bounding up to the car, with a small white Scottish terrier in eager pursuit.

'I believe the police brought Miss Kepple's little dog, Carlos, here from Addlefield Hospital?' Valda said.

'That's right. Have you come to fetch him?'

'No. I'm afraid Miss Kepple will be in hospital for a few days. I'm Sister of the ward she's in and I promised to enquire after Carlos because she was so worried about him.'

'He's a dear little chap but he hasn't settled at all well,' Miranda told her. 'I was hoping you were a friend, come to take him off my hands. I'm really full up, you see. I only agreed to take him because of the circumstances, but tomorrow I've got his kennel booked for someone else. Still, that's my problem. I've recently made an agreement with the police for these rare occasions so Carlos will have to share, I'm afraid. Anyway, come and see for yourself. How is the old lady?'

Valda bristled at the 'old lady' bit, but in spite of the girl's casual attitude Valda couldn't help liking her.

'She had her operation today. I meant to phone you to enquire after Carlos before I came off duty, but it's always hectic on theatre days. My father lives in Deasley so this isn't far out of my way. I'll phone in and leave a message that the dog's okay.'

The girl laughed. 'He isn't, actually. I appreciate that you can't tell your patient that, but he hasn't eaten today. I suspect he's thoroughly indulged so he doesn't like being one of a crowd. He needs lots of affection and attention, and I simply don't have time.'

She led the way to a kennel where a little dog lay in the corner looking miserable. Miranda opened the door and as soon as Valda spoke his name he got up hopefully. As Valda patted him she told Miranda how Miss Kepple had acquired him.

'That accounts for his behaviour,' Miranda said. 'You wouldn't—? No, you can't if you work at the hospital.'

'I'd love to have him if I was at home,' Valda began, feeling sorry for Carlos who obviously thought he was about to be let out of the kennels, then an idea flashed across her mind. 'Wait a minute,' she said, standing up to face Miranda. 'My father lives alone. He's recently retired, it would give him something to do—I wonder.' She tried to visualise her father's reaction. 'I'll have to ask him, of course.'

'Ring from the house?' Miranda suggested with a warm smile.

Valda agreed and Carlos appeared to have made up his mind as he followed close on her heels.

Miranda laughed as they walked back to the bungalow.

'He likes you,' she said. 'Dogs are funny, they either do or they don't. Myself, I like bigger dogs. I'd have kept Carlos indoors but my two reds would eat him!'

She shut them outside as she took Valda, who had picked Carlos up, into the kitchen.

Valda could only be brief on the telephone and the way she put it her father didn't have much option but to agree.

Miranda fetched Carlos's lead. 'I'm so grateful, and I'm sure Miss Kepple would much prefer him to be in a private home. She doesn't seem the type of dog-owner who would approve of kennels.'

'I'm sure it was nothing personal, Miss—?'

'Oh, call me Miranda—everyone does,' she said cheerfully. 'Do let me know how things go, and how the old girl gets on.'

'How much does Miss Kepple owe you?'

'Nothing at all—my pleasure. I only wish I could have done more.'

'But Miss Kepple would expect to pay,' Valda insisted.

'Wouldn't hear of it. After all, he's been no bother and hasn't eaten a sausage. I make my living out of the people who choose to leave their dogs and cats. Miss Kepple didn't—poor soul, she was rather forced into it. Glad to have been able to help in a crisis.'

It almost seemed to Valda that Carlos was actually laughing as he sat beside her on the front passenger seat, and in less than half an hour she pulled in through the already open five-barred gate at the side of Maple Cottage. But now Carlos's confidence wavered. At the sight of Howard Bergman he started to growl, and it was some minutes before Valda chanced to let him run loose.

'Take no notice of him, Val,' her father advised, kissing her in his usual paternal way. 'He'll come round when we feed him.'

'I only hope I've done the right thing,' Valda said with a worried frown on her face. 'Poor Miss Kepple might not like the idea. I acted on impulse, now I'm not so sure.'

'Give the hospital a ring and tell the nurse to give the poor old soul a message.'

'Hey, not so much of the poor old soul,' Valda said good-naturedly. 'I don't suppose she's so much older than you.'

Her father laughed. 'Well, you know how eccentric we all get when we get old.'

'I don't consider you old,' quipped Valda, going to the kitchen and shaking some of the dog food Miranda had supplied into a bowl she ferreted out from a cupboard. Howard Bergman went to stand by his daughter and put his arm round her shoulders.

'Brings back memories, doesn't it?' he said sadly. 'Remember how Cleo used to sit here and beg while we prepared her food?'

'I remember—but I'd rather not,' Valda replied firmly.

'I don't reckon it hurts now and again to remember the good times,' Howard said wistfully.

'If you can separate the good from the bad times, and it isn't easy.' She switched the kettle on and made some gravy to pour over the biscuits, then she looked in the fridge to see what meat was available.

'What are you looking for?' Howard asked her.

'Mm—meat. Is that cold lamb for your dinner tomorrow?'

'For both of us. I know you like cold meat and salad and that was a good-sized joint I had in the freezer so I thought I'd have a roast today, cold tomorrow.'

'Can we spare a bit for Carlos?' Valda asked hopefully.

'What's wrong with tinned dog food?'

'Not good enough for our Carlos. As Miranda said, he's rather indulged.'

Howard looked round and saw Carlos sitting in the back doorway, and he softened.

'Go on then, Val. I suppose I'll have to indulge him too if I don't want to lose a finger, or some other part of my anatomy.'

Valda followed her father's gaze and saw that Carlos was licking his lips and talking in his quaint way. Already Howard had fetched the carving knife and was adding tasty lean slivers of lamb to the dog's bowl.

'The way to a dog's heart is much the same as to a man's, I expect,' Valda said with a laugh.

'You'd know all about that I've no doubt, though I would have thought a pretty girl like you didn't need to use any cunning to get the man whose heart she's after.'

Valda only grunted and put the bowl down for Carlos who immediately attacked his supper with relish.

'How is that young man of yours by the way?' Howard added pointedly.

Valda rounded on her father with a hurt expression

in her large eyes. 'Why do you say it like that, Dad? His name is Adrian—but thanks all the same he's fine, or he was the last time I saw him.'

'Oh—like that is it? Touchy subject?'

'No! O-oh—' she flounced out of the kitchen. 'I must ring Pam on the ward.' She went, all too aware that her cheeks were glowing at the amused grin on her father's face.

He's almost gloating, she thought bitterly. He hopes we've had a tiff and he hopes he'll never see Adrian again. She dialled the hospital's number knowing that she was being unjust to her father who probably had no such hopes.

Valda gave Pam the message which was to be passed on to Miss Kepple and squirmed at the quip Pam made about getting too involved with patients. Valda realised that it was probably Sebastian Carr's concern for Miss Kepple's welfare which had prompted her actions. Later, when she watched her father and Carlos playing like old friends, she was pleased she had rescued the dog from Miranda's kennels. That was passing unfair judgment too, she reproached herself. Miranda was young, but that didn't mean that she wasn't devoted to the animals left in her care. Valda was sure she was, but a new interest was what her father needed now that he'd retired. She remained at the lounge window which looked out over the wide lawn where Carlos was chasing sticks her father was throwing.

Howard Bergman was only sixty-one, still fairly active and healthy with an alert brain and vibrant mind. He should be occupied, she thought disconsolately, or he would get bored and lazy. No, he'd never be that, the house was spotlessly clean, and he loved to cook as well as taking great pride in the garden where to one side of the house he grew all manner of vegetables. As Valda watched, Carlos rolled over for her father to rub his tummy which he did, and any fears Valda had that she had done the right thing instantly vanished. Her father was a dear and she loved him with sincere devotion. Valda was proud of him too. He was a big, handsome man, ridiculously fresh-faced for a man of his years, his ruddy coloured cheeks enhanced by the shock of wavy white hair. There was an unmistakable twinkle in his soft blue eyes even though he'd been a strict disciplinarian. When a teenager Valda had thought him unfeeling at times, but having been a police sergeant in the Bristol area for much of his working life she appreciated now the reasons for his dominance. She remembered how the twinkle had been absent, his features grey and defeated for a few long agonising years after her mother had left for Australia with a much younger man. Valda had been just sixteen, her elder brothers Richard and Ian, nineteen and twenty-one respectively, when their world of sunshine had suddenly become blackened by dark clouds of uncertainty. How could her mother have been capable of such cruelty? It was a question which even now after eight years tormented Valda, and one which would never be satisfactorily answered. Valda's clear bright eyes misted over as she felt the hurt inflicted on her father. Yet not once had he ever condemned his wife for her callousness.

Valda didn't notice that the garden had become barren of human life and she jumped when her father placed a gentle hand on her shoulder.

'What's up, lass?' he asked kindly.

Valda pursed her lips and clenched her fists angrily.

'Why, Dad, why?' she asked vehemently. 'How could *she* go off and leave all this—you—I mean, it's not as if you were ugly or beastly—or——?'

'How do you know what I was to your mother, Val?'

Valda turned sharply and looked at her father quizzically. He forced a smile, but the wry twist at the corner of his mouth betrayed a moment of self-criticism.

'Oh, Val,' he said despondently, 'I thought I was a good husband, but I must have failed somewhere.'

Valda looked down, unable to bear the hidden grief in her father's voice.

'You always said that it was no good asking questions which had no answer,' she said softly. 'Yet I fancy you've been asking the same question as me for the past eight years.'

He sighed and stretched. 'Carlos has brought back memories, my dear—memories of a loving family, laughter and happiness, memories of a tornado which tore us all apart, but we—you and me, Val, we weathered the storm, and I'm grateful for your loyalty. The question I've often asked is why did you stay with me when you could have gone to a land of sunshine and surfing, and a life of fun with your mother?'

'Maple Cottage is home—and home is *you*, Dad,' she answered firmly.

'Don't hate your mother, Val. Don't despise her, or think badly of her. She didn't set out to hurt us all, you know.'

'Then why did she do it, Dad?' Valda flashed angrily at the big man who was everything to her. Comforter, protector and friend.

'I still don't really know, Val. Maybe she was too young at nineteen when I married her. Perhaps she wasn't ready for settling down and having a family so young.'

'She was twenty-one by the time Ian was born—it's not *that* young,' Valda argued.

'Not by today's standards, love—yet, here you are, twenty-four, and still not married.'

Valda immediately saw that her father was leading up to something so she said nothing.

'Wouldn't you like to explore the world a bit, Val?' he pursued. 'Go and spend a year with your mother perhaps?'

'Good heavens, *no*!' Now Valda's cheeks were flushed with impatience. 'If I never see her again it'll be too soon,' she said crossly. 'What are you trying to do? Get rid of me?'

Howard Bergman laughed and drew Valda close against his massive chest.

'You know better than that, my girl. What I'm trying to say, Val, is that if some job comes up—abroad—anywhere, and you feel like taking off, then do it. Go, my dear, while you've got the chance, and you'll have my blessing.'

Valda was silent. Just what was he trying to say? There was some hidden connotation behind his suggestion she was sure. Slowly she turned to face him.

'You don't like Adrian, do you?' she blurted. 'So you think if I go away it'll end the affair. Why, Dad? Are you afraid I'm going to make the same mistake you and Mum made?'

Her father raised an eyebrow and his features became lined with the severity of authority she remembered of old.

'If you were a few years younger, lass—and me as well—I reckon I'd have reacted violently to a kidney punch like that.'

'That's evading the question,' she retorted pertly.

'All right then—I don't want to see you marry the first chap who comes along—you haven't seen the world yet, Val. You've worked hard, you're the best daughter a man could have, I'm proud of you, but I want you to be happy because I care.'

'Oh, Dad,' Valda cried, and flinging her arms around his neck she let her tears spill over between their cheeks which were pressed close together.

There was no reason for tears except that she didn't exchange all this emotional sob-stuff with her father every day. He let her weep—for all she knew he might have been shedding a tear too—then he patted her affectionately and whispered, 'There's plenty of hot water. You smell of hospitals; go and have a bath, then we'll have a night-cap.'

In one way she was glad to escape, but she lay in the warm water and reflected over much of what had happened during the past three years. She knew she had her father to thank for getting through Finals when she was barely twenty-one. He'd encouraged in every way possible and afterwards had refused to let her live at home permanently because he felt the travelling would tire her out. He'd helped her to buy her own small car so that she could go home at weekends or days off if she wanted to. And she had always wanted to. Maple Cottage was the perfect place to relax. It was set in a quarter of an acre of ground with few near neighbours, just fields and a paddock, the last remaining link with the fine old stately home where her grandfather had been head gardener and which was now an exclusive, expensive nursing home. Her early childhood had been spent in Addlefield where her father had been given the privilege of a police-house, but later when his parents died, because of his connections with the big house he had been able to buy their small cottage and some land in Deasley. They had continued to live in Addlefield, but holidays and weekends all the family had worked together to renovate and modernise Maple Cottage, having extensions built on which were in keeping with the period of the cottage.

After all the work her mother had put into it how could she just up and leave everybody? The memory of that grey November day when Valda had returned home from school and found the three-bedroomed detached house in Addlefield deserted would stay with her for ever. At first she didn't suspect anything, but had got on with her homework believing that her mother had gone to check on Maple Cottage, but when she began to look about for signs of the prepared evening meal, the emptiness, the desolation of being cast off had made her grow cold with fear. There was no evening meal prepared, and when Richard didn't come in from work Valda had sensed something was wrong. She phoned

Maple Cottage several times but there was no reply, and as panic increased she had rushed to her parents' bedroom where she found the drawers and wardrobe empty. Finally, in desperation Valda had phoned her father at the police station. In disbelief he returned home at once but Valda had watched his spirit break as every effort to trace his wife failed. And Richard—her own brother—how could he have been party to such a dreadful act? He and their mother had always been close—he was the chosen one whom Jeanne Bergman couldn't bear to leave behind, and it was only later that they learned that Richard's boss was the man who had caused the break up of a once happy family. Valda suspected that her father had willed himself to carry on in the hope that one day his wife and son would simply walk back into Maple Cottage. But Valda felt bitter; only she knew that her father's agony had resulted in a heart condition.

A bang on the door startled Valda.

'Are you drowning in there?' her father called. 'The water must be cold.'

'I'm just coming,' Valda called back. The water was barely tepid. Not that she had started off with it very hot as the night was warm. She almost always showered in the Sister's Home so a long, leisurely bath was a luxury only Maple Cottage could provide.

A few minutes later she perched on the window seat in the lounge, her father sitting facing her in a huge recliner chair, a present from his colleagues on his retirement a few months ago. She looked cautiously into his face searching for signs of weariness, but his twinkle was back, and the creases at the corners of his eyes were white compared with the sunburn on the rest of his face.

'You've caught the sun,' Valda observed lightly.

'Good—I mean to make the most of any good weather that comes along. You ought to be spending your time off at the beach.'

Valda shrugged. 'Can't be bothered with the hassle of getting to the coast,' she said. 'I can sunbathe in the garden, but I don't want to get burnt.'

'It's the fresh air you need, m'dear, cooped up in that hospital twenty-four hours a day.'

'I go out during my off duty, Dad. What's on tomorrow? Is there anything needs doing?'

'Nope.' He sounded very adamant, Valda noticed. She also glimpsed the smile which played around his mouth, which he wasn't quite successful in concealing.

'Dad—what are you up to?'

He put on a look of mock surprise. 'Me? Nothing—I was just thinking.'

'About what?'

'Mm—Carlos,' he said, suddenly noticing the little dog at his feet.

'Dad,' Valda reproved. 'There *is* something—I know—a *woman*! Have you found yourself a lady friend?' she implored, intrigued.

Her father threw his head back in instantaneous laughter.

'Bless you, no! Haven't I got enough trouble with you? Save me from women—there's plenty in the village who'd just love to get an invitation to Maple Cottage.'

Valda studied him silently, then said seriously: 'You ought to get married again, Dad. You need a companion.'

'Well not any of Deasley's wealthy spinsters, thank you.'

They both laughed in amused recognition of the spindly Miss James who sometimes baked him a cake. Then there was young Mrs Barker whom her father always called the 'merry widow' who managed to find numerous little household jobs she couldn't manage, after eight o'clock in the evening.

'They all mean well, Dad,' Valda said earnestly.

Howard Bergman lit up his pipe and then leaned forward eagerly.

'You know the people who moved into Home Farm a while back?' He hardly waited for Valda to nod before he continued: 'Nice couple, Mr and Mrs Forbes, but he died, you know, about six months ago.'

'Who's there now then?' Valda asked, only vaguely interested.

'Appears Mrs Forbes is carrying on by herself.'

'Oh, *I* see,' Valda responded knowingly. 'She's won you over where all the other ladies have failed.'

'You've got a one-track mind, young lady. Give me credit for a little discretion. She's still pretty cut up about losing her husband. No—she's managing very well with the help of a stock-man, but you remember how they used to sell their strawberries at market, well, this year she's opened up the field and you can go and pick your own.'

'Good idea,' Valda said non-committally. 'Most farmers are doing that nowadays.'

'I thought you might like to go over tomorrow morning and pick some.'

'Yes, all right,' she agreed. 'I'll get some cream too while I'm there. That's if they still do it.'

'Oh yes, everything's carrying on much as it was before. She's a courageous woman, I'll say that for her.'

Valda finished her drink then took the beakers out to the large square kitchen. A few minutes later her father called that he was going to take Carlos for a short walk before turning in, so Valda went to bed and had fallen asleep before they returned. Her last thoughts had been of Adrian. Soon they'd be together. She was hoping he'd get over for lunch, so she'd have to be up early to pick the strawberries. They would all enjoy them for tea and then, Valda knew, Adrian would be impatient to leave Maple Cottage. They'd go to his flat and spend the evening making up for all the times when they could only smile politely or exchange a few words. Why was it that the image of Adrian caressing her body faded and for no reason she could think of the new consultant pushed his way into her mind?

Valda woke from force of habit next morning at six-thirty with strawberries on her mind. The sun already reflected a pale glow through the curtains, but she turned over, remembering that it was Sunday and she couldn't pick strawberries this early. She slept for another hour and had been lying awake listening to distant country sounds from outside, the sound of her father creeping downstairs and the kettle whistling from the kitchen before a gentle knock sounded on the door.

'Hope I'm not disturbing you, Val?' her father whispered as he opened the door and padded across the shaggy pile carpet in his slippers, placing a small tray on her bedside table. 'Had a good night?'

'Mm,' Valda murmured as she sat up. 'How's Carlos been?' she asked as she heard a whine from downstairs.

'Good as gold. He slept on an old piece of blanket in the back porch. He's had a drink of milk, now I'm going to dress and take him for a walk before breakfast.'

'Don't be long then,' Valda said. 'I'll cook breakfast and then I'll go and get those strawberries before Adrian arrives.'

'Coming to lunch then is he?'

'If he's free. He'll ring first I expect.'

Valda's father went off and Valda got out of bed and drew back the curtains. She opened the casement window and filled her lungs full of sweet fresh air before drinking her cup of tea. After a quick wash she put on a revealing tee-shirt and some very brief tight-fitting shorts—really old jeans which she had cut off and frayed at the lower edge of the legs to form a fringe. When her father and Carlos returned the kitchen was inviting with a delicious smell of bacon, sausages and tomatoes grilling.

'Spoiling me again, I see,' her father said.

'By the amount of food in the fridge and freezer you do a very good job of spoiling yourself,' she quipped.

Carlos too was spoilt as he sat between them in the dining alcove off the kitchen, looking hopefully from one to the other, and later as Valda watched her father and the little dog she wondered whether her good intentions hadn't been misguided. How was he going to feel when Carlos had to go home to Miss Kepple? She'd have to give the matter serious thought before his next birthday. He'd enjoy the challenge of training a puppy. It would be good company as well as forcing him to keep active.

When she'd washed up and tidied the kitchen she set off down the garden and over the ranch-style fence into the paddock. Carlos followed her for a few yards but Howard Bergman was too appealing to the little dog and he quickly returned to his foster master.

When Valda reached the strawberry field she found she was not the first to arrive. People were already picking and two teenage boys were handing out the punnets. They looked at Valda, then at each other with a smirk, and it wasn't until Valda had taken two punnets and walked up between rows of strawberry plants that she realised it was her type of dress which had caused the critical looks. Her tee-shirt was sleeveless with a low vee-neck, made of the kind of cotton knit which could be worn without a bra, but she concentrated on filling the punnets with as big strawberries as she could find, rather than dwell on how men reacted to her body. Occasionally she couldn't resist the temptation of popping a strawberry into her mouth and just when her mouth was full of juice a voice said: 'Pinching the profits, Sister Bergman?'

CHAPTER THREE

VALDA gulped and spluttered at the accusing masculine voice. It was much later that she realised it wasn't just the masculine voice which had startled her but the fact that she recognised it. Furious for being caught in the act she glanced up and found Sebastian Carr gazing down at her.

'Is there a law against eating the odd one or two?' she asked, shading guilty eyes by fluttering her eyelids.

He was laughing, his gleaming white teeth dazzling in the sun.

'We'll let you off,' he said, stooping down on his haunches to look straight into her face.

She had taken in at a glance that he was wearing jeans and a short-sleeved shirt. It was of the knitted cotton variety with navy blue flashes on the shoulders.

'*You'll* let me off?' she asked stupidly. What could it have to do with him she wondered, when he must be here as a customer too.

'I have a vested interest in the place since my brother-in-law died,' he explained. 'Didn't your father tell you?'

Valda stood up. 'No, he did not!' she said fiercely. 'And *you* didn't tell me you knew my father!'

He surveyed her mockingly as he too stood up straight.

'No, I chose not to. I thought your father would explain. Didn't you wonder how I knew all about Sister Bergman, the Nordic beauty, and where to find her?'

'Nordic beauty?' she echoed, a trifle annoyed that he dared to use one of her father's favourite expressions.

Sebastian nodded, and inclined his head. 'A perfect description which your father used so that I would recognise his darling daughter. With a name like

Bergman, and colouring such as yours, blonde, blue-
eyed, what origins could you have other than Germanic?
Don't look so upset—I'll try to keep the term between
ourselves.'

A retort that he didn't have the right to use it at all
rushed to her lips, but that would be a sure fire way for
him to torment her, so she bent down to continue
picking strawberries.

Sebastian helped her.

'You don't have to,' Valda began, wishing he'd go
away, wishing that she was more suitably dressed to
meet one of the senior staff from the hospital.

'I want to,' he said as if it was the most natural thing
to do. 'I promised your father some good big strawberries so when we've filled these two punnets we'll go up
to the house and get the ones I've kept especially for
him.'

'I didn't know Dad was *that* fond of strawberries,'
Valda said.

'Actually he said it was you who are particularly fond
of them.'

Valda couldn't think of anything to say. But she'd
have something to say to that father of hers when she
got home!

For a few moments they picked in silence, then Valda
asked: 'How did you come to meet Dad then?'

'Where else but in the inn, the obvious place to go
and meet the locals. Jessica and Frank were enjoying
life here in Deasley. I don't know that Jess is going to
be able to carry on alone, but I like the area too so
when the opportunity of a consultancy cropped up at
Addlefield I thought it was just right.'

'You live with your sister?'

'Heavens, no! Well, not if I can help it, but at present
I'm trying to help her without antagonising her, and
she seems to think I'm much too useless in practical
matters to cope alone so I'm trying to keep the peace.
During this busy period she can do with any help

available, even mine, so I spend much of my free time here. The fresh air does me good. It's important for people like us who work inside all the time to get as much as possible. You're a lucky young lady being able to come home to such a lovely spot.'

Valda just smiled, her thoughts of pique still aimed towards her father who she realised had engineered this particular meeting as well as informing the new consultant that his daughter just happened to be one of Addlefield's nursing sisters.

As soon as the punnets were filled Valda stood up, Sebastian taking the punnets from her. She followed him through the narrow track between the plants noticing that a queue had formed at the weigh-in and pay counter, but Sebastian turned in the opposite direction. He paused at a gap in a high hedge, looked over his shoulder to make sure that Valda was following and with a curt, 'Come on,' proceeded through the hedge along a wider path where vegetables were growing in orderly rows on either side. At a tall wrought iron gate in the next hedge he waited for Valda to open the latch and then they were in a well laid out flower and shrub garden with a curving pathway of paving stones leading to the back of the house.

'Look, I really must pay for the strawberries,' Valda hesitantly protested. 'They should have been weighed.'

'Stop wittering,' Sebastian muttered and walked briskly to a side porch and into a large modern kitchen.

Somehow Jessica Forbes was not quite the person Valda had imagined her to be. She was bending down at the oven, basting a good-sized turkey as they entered. If Sebastian Carr was in his mid-thirties Valda had presumed that his sister would be older, nearer forty. 'Frank' had sounded at least forty-five to her if not fifty, but the attractive red-head who stood up with graceful agility was no more than thirty years old. Valda realised that there could have been a sizeable age difference between Mr and Mrs Forbes. There had been twelve years between her own parents she remembered.

'So you're Howard's daughter?' Jessica said when Sebastian had made a cursory introduction. There was a dominant tone in her voice which Valda didn't care for. Beautiful though she was—no not beautiful, Valda corrected, certainly attractive—there was a hard look about her regular features. For a red-head she was very well tanned, her arms and legs long and obvious as she wore only brief cotton shorts and tee-shirt in pale green. She had dark hazel eyes which were definitely sizing up Valda's appearance. 'And you're going to be Sebastian's number one assistant?' she added with a hint of sarcasm.

Valda laughed weakly. 'Hardly that! We have a considerable staff at the hospital.'

'I didn't mean professionally, though as Sister-in-charge of eye wards you'll be that as well—no, I meant in his campaign to raise money.'

Valda looked at her new boss with indignation. 'I haven't agreed to anything,' she said.

Sebastian's warm smile only made her bristle more.

'Your father has been telling me how you've laboured tirelessly in the past for a local orphanage,' he said. 'Most impressive dedication to a worthy cause, and one which I heartily endorse and will support. My appeal though won't be a long lasting one—just a summer of good effort to raise the required sum. The inn are having a darts marathon and the church have agreed on a special jumble sale and fête, so we really must put ourselves out to show that we can do our share. More than our share, in fact. I intend that the staff on eye wards should raise the largest amount of money.'

'How, for goodness' sake?'

'Sponsored swims and walks. We're fortunate in a way because our patients are mostly short stay—less than a week in many cases—so we should get lots of patients interested during the next few months.'

'I think it all sounds a bit over-ambitious,' Valda said.

'You father assured me that you'd be all for it,' Sebastian told her.

'He can't speak for me. He knows I work long hours, and spend a great deal of my off duty visiting him.'

'Perhaps more than you need.'

Valda pulled herself up to her full height, then too late realised that she had drawn attention to her long bare legs which by Sebastian's expression he fully approved of. How dare he suggest that her father didn't need her! She wanted to yell back at him, but being a guest in his sister's house she kept control of her temper.

'Perhaps Valda has other interests,' Jessica said kindly. 'A young and attractive girl like her probably has a string of admirers.'

'No, only one.' Valda felt her cheeks glow, annoyed with herself for revealing anything about her private life, but no doubt her father had told these people far too much.

'Then we must rope him in as well,' Sebastian said.

'He's a very busy GP,' Valda put in quickly.

Nothing, but nothing was going to daunt the enthusiasm of this crusader. 'At the practice in Addlefield? I've probably met him, and all the staff there are keen to help us.'

Valda felt trapped, conned, but she dared to take a fleeting glimpse at Sebastian. She wasn't sure she could handle this man's dictatorship, so very different from his predecessor who had recently been appointed to a teaching post in a London eye clinic. He had been the reserved, unassuming type of man but devoted to his work. Sebastian Carr seemed to be undermining her position, and her will. She felt as if not only had the Eye Unit been taken over but her personality as well. She refused to let it happen in spite of her heartbeats thudding like jungle drums, beating out a rhythm, a tortuous signal.

'I . . . I think I ought to be going,' she murmured, trying to moisten the cruel dryness in her mouth which threatened to suffocate her.

'I can count on you then?' Sebastian said smoothly. 'You and your staff, let's make it a real team effort, eh?'

'When I know more about what you have in mind maybe I'll consider it, but at present, Mr Carr, I'm not prepared to commit myself.'

Jessica glanced up from her cooking. 'Been here all of twenty-four hours and not on first name terms yet?' she asked her brother.

'Plenty of time, isn't there, Valda? Not everyone can bring themselves to use mine, but once you've said it, it isn't so bad. Try saying it to yourself several times before you go to sleep—beats counting sheep.'

'Take no notice of him, Valda, he's teasing you. He's aiming to chalk you up as another of his conquests and I don't mean in his crusade. He has an unbeatable record of breaking hearts and scattering the pieces over acres of virgin soil.'

'As I said, I already have a boy-friend,' Valda replied quickly, meaning to sound unimpressed, but her words lacked credibility.

'You and Howard must come over to lunch one day,' Jessica suggested.

'Why not today? That turkey is large enough to feed an army,' Sebastian said.

'Thank you, that's very kind of you but I'm expecting Adrian.'

'For lunch?' Sebastian prompted.

'As far as I know.' She wasn't terribly good at lying and in her heart even though she was preparing for Adrian to arrive by lunchtime, she doubted that he would. Sometimes she wondered whether he considered a country cottage too lowly a place to stay long. Or was it professional etiquette, having visited and treated her father which prevented him from visiting Maple Cottage socially? The most likely reason, she knew, was her father's attitude which Valda realised made them both feel awkward. It wasn't that he wasn't pleasant to Adrian, he was, but his manner of indifference inhibited them.

Valda thanked Jessica again for the invitation to lunch, tried to insist on paying for the strawberries which was adamantly refused and Sebastian held on to the basket.

'I'll walk you back,' he said. 'I really am anxious to discuss ideas to raise money with you.'

'I'm sure I should be flattered that you've asked my help, Mr Carr,' she said firmly. 'but I honestly don't think that I can get involved.'

'Involved!' He spoke tersely. 'My dear girl, you're that already. You disappoint me, Valda. By all accounts I didn't need to win *you* round for the cause.'

Valda couldn't take his imperious stare. She curtained her eyes with fluttering lashes and switched her gaze to the ground.

'I . . . I don't mean I won't help,' she stammered, unsure of herself. 'I will when I can, but . . .' the words petered out simply because she couldn't find an excuse. 'Well, anyway,' she added, tossing her head significantly, 'thanks for the invitation to lunch and the strawberries, but I must go.'

She turned and hurried away, knowing that Sebastian Carr was glaring indignantly at her back.

She was glad of the walk to cool her flushed cheeks and steady her hammering heartbeats. She had almost fallen under his spell but there was Adrian, and as soon as she entered Maple Cottage she asked her father if he had telephoned.

'Yes, love, and he expects to be here about three.'

She refrained from making any immediate comment to her father about meeting Sebastian or being invited to lunch, but her spirits lifted a little as she prepared their meal and when he came in to wash his hands she confronted him.

'Oh, yes,' she said slowly with a touch of severity,

'you might have told me you had met Mr Carr.'

Her father kept his back to her. 'I thought he'd have mentioned that we'd met.'

'You've got a cheek,' Valda reproached, 'letting him think I'd jump at the chance to help him in this fund-raising idea of his.'

'You can't *not* help, love. You are the Sister in charge of eye wards, after all.'

'I do like to make my own decisions, Dad. He's a consultant by the way, and the nursing staff *don't* get friendly with the hierarchy.'

'Oh, I see, he's a "yes, sir", "no, sir" man is he?'

'Very definitely, so don't go speaking for me again.'

'Did you remember the cream?' When he chose, Howard Bergman was an expert at changing the subject.

'No, I forgot. Hardly surprising as he was the last person I expected to find on Home Farm. He insisted he'd picked the best strawberries for you, so I had to go to the house and meet Mrs Forbes. They invited us to lunch, she was cooking a turkey, but I made our apologies and told them that Adrian was coming.'

'Pity Adrian didn't ring earlier then we could have accepted. You'll like Mrs Forbes, and you'd have had the chance to get to know her and her brother better.'

Valda went to the cutlery drawer and hid her flushed cheeks from her father's watchful eye. She guessed he was way ahead of her in matchmaking—anything to put Adrian off—but now that she was aware of her father's acquaintanceship with Sebastian Carr she could call a halt to any schemes he was making.

'I shall see all I need to see of the crusading consultant at the hospital thank you, Dad,' she replied shortly, and hoped that put an end to Sebastian as a topic of conversation.

As they ate Valda made a point of asking about various people in the small village community where her father was becoming a target for being invited on this committee or that. Valda was pleased for him, knowing that such interests were important provided he didn't overdo it.

After lunch when he went up to his room to rest Valda asked: 'Ought I to take Carlos for a run?'

'No, I'll take him out when I get up. Give you and Adrian a bit of time to yourselves.'

'You won't get too attached to him, will you?' Valda asked with concern.

'Who, Adrian?'

'Carlos, of course,' she answered back impatiently.

'I mustn't, must I?' and her father went slowly up the stairs.

Valda cleared away in the kitchen and then went upstairs herself to have a shower before settling herself on a rug in the garden to sunbathe in her briefest bikini. Carlos had been content so far to follow Howard almost everywhere he went, but now he wriggled to get a few inches of rug close to Valda. She lay on her back soaking up the glorious warmth of the sun, trying to forget the morning's incidents to concentrate on anticipating Adrian's arrival. But the surprise of finding Sebastian Carr at Home Farm refused to be obliterated. Even more disturbing was the fact that he had struck up such a bond already with her father. Valda knew that whatever she did now, wherever she went, would be passed on, albeit unwittingly to the new consultant. What did that matter, she asked herself? It would not make one iota of difference to her life but inwardly she knew that his appearance on the scene, whether at Addlefield Eye Unit, or home at Deasley, had already created a disturbing influence. It simply didn't do to have close relationships with colleagues as she had discovered in the past. Young aspiring doctors or male nurses seldom stayed long in one hospital as ambition lured them away to seek promotion. Sebastian Carr though had just reached an important point in his life—the point at which he could be reasonably satisfied with the progress made in his career which now enabled him to sit back and enjoy some degree of social life. It was high time he had a wife, and Valda guessed that such was his quest. There was Jessica though. Where did she feature in his plans? Did he feel he had a duty where his sister was concerned, or had Sebastian decided to come to Deasley so that his sister could approve of whoever he chose for a wife? Remembering the clinical way Jessica Forbes had surveyed Valda the latter seemed the most probable reason, and that *she* was unsuitable had been made abundantly clear by the jibe about his record of breaking hearts. In the singular that would have been excusable, but the plural gave rise to suspicion that he was something of a wolf. Or was that Jessica's ace to ward off those whom she considered as unlikely candidates for the role of sister-in-law? As if it mattered one way or another to her, Valda reproached herself crossly. Sebastian Carr meant nothing to her. What better man could she have than Adrian, and as the sun made her sleepy she dozed, her fingers smoothing her silky skin in happy expectation of Adrian's visit . . .

Carlos's low growl woke Valda and by the time she had opened her eyes and got to her feet he had gone racing to the five-barred gate, a small, agitated bundle of aggression.

Valda called to him and ran round the side of Maple Cottage to find Adrian leaning on the top of the gate looking somewhat shaken.

'Hullo, darling,' Valda greeted eagerly, as always immediately captivated by Adrian's good looks.

'What's this then? A guard dog now?'

Valda clapped her hands to keep Carlos back as she helped Adrian to open the gate. It went right back to meet the corner of the cottage so that the little dog was safely netted into a patch of garden.

Valda held her lips up to Adrian for a kiss but of necessity it was sweet and brief so that Adrian could get his car in off the narrow lane. Valda closed the gate again and Carlos attacked Adrian's car with renewed

ferocity so that Valda was forced to hold him down
until Adrian got out of the car.

'He'll get used to you in a minute,' she assured Adrian
as the dog growled in self-defence.

'I hope so,' Adrian laughed, 'or I shall really believe
I'm not welcome here.'

Valda looked directly into Adrian's face with a
measure of disquiet. It was one thing for her to be
aware of and scold her father for his attitude, but it
grieved her to hear Adrian make light of the fact as if
he didn't care.

She hurriedly explained how she had rescued Carlos
from Miranda's kennels.

'I don't see why you should have got involved, Val,'
Adrian said as they walked together back to the lawn.

'I felt sorry for Miss Kepple, and as you can guess
Dad's pleased to have Carlos. He'll take him for a walk
when he gets up—to give us some time together, so he
promised.' Valda's eyes sparkled impishly at Adrian
who put his arm around her shoulders and whistled
appreciatively at her bikini-clad body. This gesture was
met with distinct disapproval by Carlos who followed
cautiously, still growling in a low, mistrustful way at
Adrian's heels.

Adrian was looking particularly attractive in light,
summery trousers and a green and white striped shirt
with short sleeves, which showed off the tawny-coloured
skin of his arms and chest. Valda pulled him down on
to the rug, caressing his arm and then recklessly sliding
one hand into the opening of his shirt.

'You're getting deliciously brown,' she purred softly.

Adrian laughed and held her close. 'You make me
sound like a nicely-done steak.'

'Good enough to eat, darling,' she whispered back.

He pushed her down and she melted into his embrace,
secure in the assurance of his love . . .

Howard Bergman's whistle for Carlos brought the
enjoyment to an end as Valda and Adrian sat up. The

two men exchanged a few words before Howard said: 'I'll put the dog in the car and take him up on the hill for a good run. What time's tea?'

Valda looked at Adrian. 'Any plans?' she asked.

'My time is yours,' he answered with a certain reserve written in his expression.

'Somewhere between five and six then?' Valda suggested, and as this seemed to satisfy her father he went towards the garage.

Valda fetched iced drinks and Adrian followed her into the kitchen after he had removed his shirt and slacks to reveal dark red swimming trunks. They stood by the work top sipping the refreshing grapefruit squash, Valda recognising the relaxation which had descended on them since her father had driven off.

Adrian took a step nearer her and placed his half-filled tumbler down on the working surface, but Valda suddenly felt a moment of panic. She ran her finger over Adrian's lean brown body to keep him at arm's length.

'You look as if you've been to the Bahamas,' she said.

He caught her waist between his hands and drew her close.

'My magic carpet takes me there every day,' he said. 'You could come too.'

Valda placed her hands on his shoulders and looked with a searching gaze into his face.

'I've joined the new sports club in Addlefield,' Adrian explained. 'More on the outskirts really. Merle and one or two of the girls went for a complimentary session when it opened, and they gave all us men at the practice a voucher, so I've been giving it a try.'

'By your tan you've given it more than just a try,' Valda said, feeling a flash of pique that he hadn't mentioned it before.

'I went for a giggle really, but I'm fast becoming hooked. You do need to go about three times a week to get the full benefit. Why don't you join?'

'Tell me more about it,' Valda invited.

'Mm—work out in the gym, sauna, solarium, swimming-pool.'

'You know I can't swim.'

'But you'd enjoy the other amenities—table tennis, badminton, there's everything there, all under one roof. Just the place to work up an appetite.' He took a nibble at her lips, then nuzzled her ear as he whispered: 'Can we go upstairs?'

Valda pushed him away. 'No,' she said in confusion, 'Dad might come back.'

Adrian dropped his hands to his side impatiently. 'Always your Dad,' he said grudgingly.

'I thought we were going to sunbathe,' she pleaded innocently.

'*He* makes you feel guilty, doesn't he? You're never really at ease when I come to Maple Cottage.'

'Well, it is his home.'

'And hasn't he gone up on the hill to give us some time to ourselves?'

'Ye-es—but I'm sure he didn't have in mind what you have.'

Adrian grabbed her, pulling her up against his chest, his fingers tenderly caressing her back.

'He's a man isn't he—and he was young once,' Adrian said.

'I . . . I thought we were going back to your flat this evening?' Valda murmured dreamily.

Adrian kissed her forcibly. 'Is that a promise?'

'I don't make promises I might not be able to keep,' she quipped sensuously as she pulled away. 'We're wasting the sunshine.'

'Guess you're right. We get so little in this country we must make the most of it.' He picked up his drink and with his arm resting round Valda's neck propelled her out into the garden again.

Adrian was full of the new club and was eager to

persuade Valda to join.

'It's time,' she said disconsolately. 'There's no sense in wasting money. If I join and pay the annual fee, how many times am I going to use the club?

'As often as you want to.'

Valda plucked at the grass, trying to find good reasons for doing as Adrian suggested yet not wholly convinced. She couldn't imagine how he was finding the time to fit so many sessions in, and as the men's and women's gyms, saunas and solariums were separate she couldn't see the point of them going together. Adrian could swim and was a keen squash player while Valda preferred outdoor sports like netball or tennis.

'With all the laser appeal fund-raising that our new consultant is organising,' she excused, 'I can't see that I'm going to have any time for spoiling myself at a sports club.'

'You know how you're fixed and whether you'd benefit from the club,' he said indifferently. 'We've all joined now from the practice, even old Doc Caswell. I've had some good games of squash, and I feel better for the exercise. I believe your new Mr Carr is calling a meeting to organise events for the laser appeal. He's roped our practice in and I understand Merle is going to act as his organising secretary.'

Merle seemed to keep cropping up in Adrian's conversation. Valda knew she was a secretary/receptionist at the practice and now she became aware of how often Adrian talked about her. So she was to be the organising secretary for the laser appeal! That must mean that Sebastian Carr had met her and enlisted her help. Was that before or after he had asked Valda for her assistance?

'Which one is Merle?' Valda asked, trying to keep her interest to the minimum. 'Have I met her?'

'Don't think so. She's the small, pretty one who replaced the old dragon when she retired. Merle is super-efficient in everything she does so Mr Carr will have no problems.'

Valda was disappointed to hear Adrian speak so disparagingly about the now retired Miss Clayton who was anything but a dragon, but she deemed it unwise to comment. She rolled over on to her stomach and a quick glance at Adrian's happy expression and satisfied smile as he lay on the rug, his eyes closed, made her feel unsure of herself. Sebastian's arrival had started this feeling of uncertainty, and now that she had learned that Merle was a willing devotee to Sebastian's crusade as well as to Adrian's sporting and spare time activities, Valda's vulnerability increased. She didn't intend to play second fiddle to anyone, and yet here she was decidedly in the position of understudy it seemed.

CHAPTER FOUR

ADRIAN slept soundly for the remainder of the hot afternoon despite Valda's restlessness beside him. She longed for him to wake, to take her in his arms and kiss her passionately in reassurance but she guessed he was deliberately being distant since her rejection. She tried to imagine events once tea was over but they wouldn't materialise, and when Howard and Carlos returned Valda was already in the kitchen preparing tea which they would enjoy in the garden. She seemed to be surrounded by strawberries; there was a limit to what three people could devour, and although she piled them into sundae glasses there were still a lot left in the basket.

Adrian woke and jumped up when he heard the rattle of cups. He went eagerly to take the tray from Valda.

'Why didn't you call me, darling,' he said, his eyes heavy from sleep but full of admiration.

'No need to wake you. I can manage,' she answered simply.

'Wouldn't like you to burn yourself or anything,' he quipped, leaning forward to kiss her.

The old rapport was there between them and they remained gazing knowingly at each other for several seconds before Adrian carried the tray to the garden table. Tea was a long drawn-out affair as the three participants covered innumerable subjects in discussion, mostly in a light-hearted, lazy sort of way which blended into the warmth of the summer Sunday afternoon, but eventually Valda went up to her room to dress, and pack the necessary items to return to Addlefield.

'I don't seem to have done much to help you, Dad,'

she said to her father who was enjoying the coolness of the lounge as he smoked his pipe and chatted to Adrian.

'Stop worrying about me, my girl,' Howard chided good-naturedly. 'I shan't starve, I can use the washing machine and there's plenty of would-be do-gooders in Deasley.'

'Sounds as if you don't want me to come home,' Valda retorted.

'I'll worry if you don't, lass, and then I'll come looking for you at the Eye Unit. Now you take care and don't work too hard.'

'Now who's worrying?'

Howard stood up and went towards Val. 'You're the only girl I've got to worry about, my dear.' He kissed her goodbye warmly. Valda didn't know why a lump came in her throat but it always did, and she felt vexed with herself for being so childishly emotional.

Her father added a punnet of strawberries to her collection of belongings. 'I've still got plenty for myself and can always go for more. You enjoy these with your friends.'

As Howard held open the gate, Valda called: 'I'll let you know when Miss Kepple's ready to go home.'

'Tell her from me that Carlos is a good little dog and not to hurry things. He'll be no trouble—now you take care on the road.'

Valda held up her hand in acknowledgement and Adrian followed her out in his dark saloon. He always insisted on travelling behind Valda so that he could keep an eye on her. There was a fair bit of traffic through the country lanes, people returning home after enjoying the good weather at local beauty spots, and as they neared Addlefield Valda saw in her mirror that Adrian was indicating to her to turn off down a side road.

The two cars pulled in near a parade of shops on a housing estate and Adrian got out and came to Valda's window.

'We're near the club, Val. Will you come in as my guest, just to have a look around? There's a nice bar there, we can have a drink before we go on to my place.'

'Okay, if you like,' she agreed with a hesitant smile.

'I'll lead the way then.'

Valda followed him through the new one-way system which skirted the town centre. She seldom visited this end of Addlefield as she only had occasion to use the shopping centre during her limited off-duty hours, so she was surprised at the changes she encountered. There were new restaurants, a few office blocks and a large multi-storey car-park which Adrian drove into. They collected tickets and went up to the third floor to find spaces side by side, then Adrian directed the way down in the lift to take the exit which led out opposite a rather prominent building which turned out to be a hotel which accommodated the sports and health club.

Adrian presented his membership card at the desk, explaining that he had just called in to show Valda around. One of the assistants gave Valda a conducted tour of the women's gym, sauna and solarium and afterwards she met up with Adrian who took her through the games rooms, and finally they emerged into the swimming-pool area. It was larger than Valda had expected, with a high domed glass roof so that the sound of splashing water along with happy voices echoed hollowly.

There were less than a dozen people in the pool, more it appeared at one end where white plastic tables and chairs were scattered with a backdrop of imaginary palm trees. As they walked round the edge of the pool a swimmer bobbed up at the side and a girl's voice hailed Adrian.

'Come on in,' she urged.

Adrian took Valda's hand lightly.

'I've brought Val—Val, this is Merle.'

In spite of herself Valda felt her muscles stiffen with

annoyance. This was something else planned behind her back she suspected, but she managed a friendly hallo in response to the other girl's greeting.

'Do you swim?' Merle asked.

'No,' Valda replied, meeting Adrian's gaze with deliberation.

'She says she can't,' Adrian said with a grin towards the shapely swimsuited figure in the water, 'but I expect if I threw her in she'd surprise herself.'

'I struggled to do a width at school,' Valda informed them, 'but I don't call that swimming, and I'm not really interested.'

'Are you going to join the club?' Merle pursued.

'I don't think so,' Valda replied. In that instant she had made up her mind definitely not to. The feeling of uncertainty had progressed to convincing her that here she would be in the way. 'There's no point,' she went on hurriedly, 'I'd never have the time to benefit from it.'

'It's open until ten every evening, and a sauna makes you feel good; especially beneficial for you, I'd have thought, after a hard day on the wards.'

'I'll have to persuade her,' Adrian said, squeezing Valda's hand.

'Aren't you coming in for a swim, Adrian?' Merle asked again.

Adrian didn't answer as quickly as Valda thought he should have done, which prompted her to say: 'I'm sure you'd like to, darling. Time's getting on anyway, and I don't want to be late back.'

'I promised you a drink,' Adrian reminded her firmly and guided her to the door.

'There's no need, Adrian,' Valda insisted. 'I don't want to spoil your fun.'

The lounge bar was dimly lit, extensively carpeted and furnished, and Adrian went straight to the attractively styled counter and ordered a sweet sherry for Valda, a lager for himself.

'Shall we sit here or go back by the pool?' Adrian asked sharply.

'Wherever you like,' Valda said, sensing an atmosphere of antagonism.

He turned and went to the most distant table near the window. Only one elderly gentleman sat on a stool at the bar counter.

They sat opposite one another, Adrian taking a long drink before looking directly at Valda.

'My "fun" is being with you,' he said in a severe tone. 'I thought I'd been promised some fun at my flat.'

'But we aren't at your flat.'

'You're a Sister, you don't have to be in at a certain time. It's still early, we could have had a swim here, you'd find it invigorating, then back to the flat for—coffee?'

She looked across at him, his dark handsome features suggestive of all that she had desired most—once.

'I don't like the water, Adrian, I've explained all that before, so please don't try to force me into anything.'

He spread his knees wider apart round the small table and leaned forward, sliding one hand up inside the slit of her dress.

Valda had dressed to please Adrian. He constantly told her that no matter what she wore she always looked beautiful, but she liked to appear feminine for him, and she had put on a silky summer dress with a creamy coloured background in which were multi-coloured bubbles. The style was simple, sleeveless with ruching on the shoulders decorated with neat bows. The fitted bodice was laced together for a few inches above the elasticated waist, and the skirt was slightly flared with side slits.

'Force you? Have I ever tried to do that?' he asked tersely.

Valda looked away from his intense gaze. 'Well—no-o.'

'You're always so demonstrative, Val. You aim to

please, and you must know with a figure like yours a
man can only have one thought in his mind, but what
happens when we're alone and with every opportunity
to make love? You go cold on me. It's your father's
influence, he makes you feel guilty. If we'd gone straight
to the flat what would your excuse have been this time?'

'You make it all sound too serious, Adrian.'

'Isn't that what most girls are looking for? A serious
relationship?'

'It takes a while to get to know people. It isn't right
to feel committed too soon.'

She hadn't meant it to sound as if she wasn't sure of
herself but Adrian sat back, promptly severing the
contact between them. He drank in silence, finishing his
lager and placing the glass down on the coaster with a
decisive clatter.

'You seem tired and edgy today,' he accused.

'I'm fine,' Valda answered shortly.

'You want to go, I believe?' Adrian made to stand
up, then noticed that she hadn't finished her sherry. She
sipped, deliberately delaying the moment of parting
which she knew had to come.

'And you want to stay,' she said pointedly.

There was an awkward moment of tension.

'All right then, yes, I'd like a swim,' he admitted
honestly. 'I hoped I could have persuaded you.' He
laughed meaninglessly. 'Give me time, darling, this is
all a novelty which no doubt will wear off in time. At
least it keeps me fit and is an outlet for my frustration.
We both know "fun" is about all we'd have had if we'd
gone back to the flat.'

He walked her to the door. There was no need for
dishonest words like: 'I don't like staying here when
you're going back to Conifer Lodge.' He kissed her
cheek. 'Think about joining, Val. I honestly think it
would do you good.'   Valda was a bit hurt that he
didn't accompany her to the car-park, and she tried not
to imagine that it was the petite, bouncy little girl in

the pool who was the attraction. She had to acknowledge that Adrian was right about her attitudes. She enjoyed being with him, she loved to show her feelings, prove her adoration of him, but she was afraid of letting him become too amorous. She supposed she couldn't expect him to hover on the edge of the volcano for ever.

At least the evenings were light now until between nine and ten o'clock. She didn't hurry back to the car-park but mingled with people out for a stroll, church-goers returning home after the evening service, as she window-gazed in some of the new shops, deciding that she would come to this end of town on her next afternoon off. It was about half an hour later that she drove out of the car-park, then she got into the wrong lane and had to drive round the one-way system again which meant that she passed the door of the hotel and sports club. Movement on the pavement made her glance towards the elegant entrance just in time to see Adrian coming out with the pretty little brunette hanging on to his arm. Valda had to concentrate hard to get in the right lane and then she recklessly drove as fast as she dared to the other end of Addlefield and the hospital grounds.

She was thankful to bring her car to a stop in the old barn where she sat and stared miserably into space, then the thought of being alone with her misery in her own room enticed her to lock up the car and make her way across the garden to the Sisters' Home. She met Pam going on duty.

'Hallo, you're back early. Adrian been called out?' Pam asked.

'Yes,' Valda lied easily. Not exactly a lie she reflected as she unlocked the door to her room. His attractive, extrovert receptionist had done that! She tortured herself with thoughts of what they were doing. Obviously enjoying each other's company back at his flat. She had a good mind to ring him up and tell him that she had seen them leave together, but she eventually calmed down. Wasn't it, after all, her own fault that it wasn't she who was enjoying his company at his flat? She had set out so full of anticipation of being with Adrian, and now she was alone this early on a Sunday evening tormented with the certain knowledge that Adrian and Merle were together. Adrian had described his secretary/receptionist as pretty and that was the first impression one perceived. But was she physically attractive, or was it her bouncy personality? Valda didn't feel she had seen enough of her to pass judgement. At least Merle had the knack of getting involved with members of the opposite sex. Adrian and also Sebastian Carr. Valda flopped back on to her bed and felt utterly dejected. Hadn't she had her chances and thrown them away? She was able to forget Adrian and Merle as memories of Sebastian flooded back into her brain.

After a restless night Valda was up early, glad to be going on duty and admitting to herself that her clean navy blue uniform dress, crisp white apron and cap sitting atop her chic blonde hair looked good and made her feel more mature. She went along to the small kitchen on her floor to fetch the punnet of strawberries which she had decided to take to Miss Kepple. She felt she never wanted to see another strawberry herself. They would be a constant reminder of a disastrous weekend. She had listened to the night report and visited the new admissions before going to Miss Kepple's room.

'That looks hopeful, Miss Kepple,' Valda greeted cheerfully, finding the patient up and sitting in an easy chair. She was pale but elegantly dressed in an oatmeal skirt with a brightly patterned silk blouse which had long sleeves and a tie-neck. There was a faint aroma of expensive perfume in the room and even with the use of only one eye she had successfully applied a delicate amount of make-up which made her look younger than her sixty-two years.

'Sister Bergman, my dear, how nice to have you back on duty again,' Miss Kepple said warmly. 'How very kind you've been too—fancy going to so much trouble to rescue my darling Carlos from the kennels.'

'It was no trouble, Miss Kepple, and after all it was the least I could do when I forgot to phone Miranda. My father lives in Deasley so it wasn't out of my way to call and see how Carlos was settling in. He is a pet so I twisted Dad's arm to have him.'

'I do hope it hasn't put your father out?'

'Not at all, it'll give him something to do and make certain that he gets the regular exercise he should have. Mind you, I'm sure Miranda was looking after Carlos admirably. She's full up, which was really why I asked Dad to have him. People wouldn't go to her if she wasn't good with their pets.'

Miss Kepple cast a doubtful frown towards Valda. 'It's money, my dear. Everyone has an ulterior motive these days, no one does anyone a good turn any more unless there's something in it for themselves. It's a rare thing to find someone who's as caring as you and your father.'

'Put it down to being country born and bred, Miss Kepple, and look at these—picked by my own fair hand at Home Farm yesterday. I just couldn't eat another strawberry so I thought it might make up in some small way for you not having any family to visit you.'

Tears sprang to Miss Kepple's eye. 'What a thoughtful girl. Your parents must be proud of you, Sister.'

Valda laughed. 'Sometimes, I expect.' She went on to explain a little about her family. Not because she wanted to divulge personal details, but because she didn't want Miss Kepple to become distressed. It was plain to see that she wasn't a depressive, or indulgent in self-pity. She was used to living alone and enjoyed her independence, but she readily admitted that she had always had a horror of illness and hospitals, and she did seem a lonely sort of person.

'I won't go so far as to say I shall ever be brave,' she confessed, 'but I shall always remember with gratitude all the kindness I've been shown here. It's all so much more homely and personal than I'd been led to believe. That lovely Mr Carr, I couldn't have come at a better time than when he'd just taken up the consultancy here, could I?'

'We pride ourselves on having the best surgeons,' Valda said with a smile. 'Now I must get on. I'm not sure whether Mr Carr will be round today, but his registrar, Mr Pyke, will see you later on.'

Valda continued on her round of all the patients in her care and half-way through dressings Ray Pyke arrived to see the new admissions.

It was two days later when Sebastian Carr made a surprise visit to the wards after a day in theatre, and Valda was immediately on her guard. Consultants usually called to do a round in the morning she thought crossly as she followed the young first-year nurse who had come to fetch her from the day room where she had been chatting to Miss Kepple and other patients there; why did he have to be different!

He was standing near the window in her office, hands in his pockets, gazing out at the view towards the hills.

'Good evening, Mr Carr, I'm sorry to keep you waiting,' Valda apologised politely.

Sebastian turned round slowly and remained with his back to the window so that she couldn't see his face clearly, and the westward setting sun glared uncomfortably in Valda's eyes.

'That's all right, Sister,' he said in a low voice.

She moved to her desk so that she was out of the direct sunlight and she could see that he was smiling gently. She couldn't imagine why but inwardly she prayed that he wouldn't mention Adrian, who was never far from her thoughts, but whereas once they had been happy, loving thoughts now she kept trying to forget him. She was hurt that he hadn't phoned or called in, and several times she had been tempted to pick up her telephone but had quelled the desire to make contact, remembering how he had left her on Sunday evening. No doubt Merle was occupying all his time, she thought irritably.

'Everything all right, Sister?' Sebastian Carr walked slowly towards her desk and she had a fleeting glimpse again of his sensuous body movements.

'Yes. Mr Pyke saw the new admissions. He hasn't put Mr Stanford down for surgery yet, nor Mrs Oxford, he wanted you to see them first.'

'Thank you, Sister, I've had several consultations with my registrar and housemen. I was enquiring after your personal welfare.'

Valda looked across at him, a sudden wave of elation washing over her. She opened her mouth to speak, then closed it again as her subconscious warned her against his flattering interest.

'Everything is fine,' she said at length as Sebastian seemed to be waiting for a reply.

He rested his hands on the desk so that his face drew level—dangerously level—with hers. The jacket of his dark blue suit was open and when he moved she heard the faint chink of his watch chain as it dangled forward. She was very conscious of him and kept her eyes lowered to the folders of notes on the desk, knowing that he was taking his fill of her femininity. She knew she dared not draw in her breath or it would accentuate her bosom which was already prominent enough owing to the tight waistband of her dress and apron. With silent deliberation Valda picked up the folders and backed away from her side of the desk. Immediately Sebastian walked round to her, standing only a hair's breadth away.

'We're holding a meeting in the lecture room at eight-thirty tomorrow evening. I hope I can count on you to be there,' he said.

Valda hesitated. How could she admit that she

desperately wanted to be anywhere that he was? Some quick thinking assured her that she wasn't admitting to anything by simply agreeing to be at a meeting for all the staff.

'I'll try,' she said softly.

'I'm counting on you to do better than that,' he said sharply, and a sly glance at his expression warned her of the speed with which he could change moods. 'We shall all have to make the utmost effort to make a go of this appeal, Sister. I'm sure you appreciate the value of laser treatment, and the benefits patients will derive from it.'

'Yes, of course—it's just that—'

'I know—time,' he interrupted. 'You don't feel that you can give up precious time allotted to that young man of yours. As a member of Addlefield's new sports and health centre he is already committed to help, so you may even get to see more of him than previously.'

Valda didn't reply, but began to walk slowly to the door. If he only knew, she thought, Merle and her club had already claimed much of Adrian's interest so it wasn't likely that he intended to put himself out for the laser appeal.

Sebastian walked close beside her as they visited the single rooms, once used as private wards. It was easy to see that this man was going to be popular with his patients. He had the knack of making each person feel special. He gave the impression that he was devoting all his knowledge, time, and energy to them and even Valda was surprised at the amount of patience he exercised as he chatted to them, encouraging them to talk to him and ask questions.

When they reached Miss Kepple's room they found her dozing in her chair, but she opened her good eye and began fussing to rearrange her hair and clothes when she realised she had company.

'I find it irksome to be confined to doing almost nothing,' she said. 'It's not that I'm not grateful, Mr

Carr, everyone has been so kind.'

'So you won't give us too bad a reputation when you go home then?' Sebastian said in his usual charming manner.

'I shall sing your praises loud and clear,' she replied, smiling back at the consultant with adulation.

He took his time examining Miss Kepple's eye, then announced that he was pleased with her progress.

'I know you want to go home, but I'd like you to stay with us for another couple of days, and when you do get home it means taking life slowly and carefully, and absolutely no bending. Let the work go for the next month.'

'As long as I'm home with my little dog I shall be happy, and I will follow your instructions, Mr Carr. I really am grateful, especially to Sister Bergman who personally saw that Carlos was being well cared for.'

Sebastian was writing in Miss Kepple's folder but Valda noticed a little smile puckering the corners of his mouth.

'You'd like to show your gratitude I expect, Miss Kepple,' he said, looking directly at her as he tucked his pen away in his inside pocket.

'I wish I knew how,' Miss Kepple said, full of interest.

'We're starting an appeal to get a special machine for treating cases like yours,' Sebastian told her. 'It means that with laser treatment we could have treated you in Outpatients—there wouldn't have been any need to stay in hospital. In the long term, of course, this means that hospital beds will be more readily available for more serious eye diseases, but I'm afraid we need a lot of money.'

Miss Kepple looked embarrassed. 'I . . . I'm afraid I don't have much money,' she began, and then Sebastian laughed, just when Valda was thinking what an unfeeling, thoughtless brute he was.

'We aren't going to make you buy us our laser machine, Miss Kepple,' he said jovially, 'but if you did feel you could help in a small way we're organising a fund-raising appeal and no gift will be refused. We shall be doing lots of things like sponsored swims—now perhaps you'd like to sponsor our delectable Sister here to swim so many lengths of the pool at the new club in Addlefield. They're very keen to help us. How about it, Sister, ten lengths?'

'I'm afraid if you rely on my swimming, Mr Carr, the appeal will never get off the ground—literally. I can't swim.'

Sebastian turned to look at Valda, first with disbelief, then his expression changed to one of amusement.

'We can soon remedy that,' he said pointedly, then: 'Ah, I remember—your particular talents lie in sprinting, I believe your father said.'

'That was back in my schooldays,' she informed him pertly.

'No reason not to take it up again. Lovely summer weather, light evenings, we can all get involved in one way or another.'

'I shall be delighted to sponsor you, Sister,' Miss Kepple offered eagerly, and Sebastian explained to her about the forthcoming meeting.

'We shall have notices on display anywhere and everywhere. The press will be asked to publicise in a big way and, of course, each member of the staff will have their own personal sponsorship form for which they will be responsible.' He smiled warmly, and flashed Valda a triumphant, gloating look. 'My appeals don't usually go unnoticed,' he added.

It crossed Valda's mind, as he was saying goodbye to Miss Kepple, that the appeal would very much be his. She doubted that anyone else's suggestions would be welcome as the whole thing was sewn up as far as Sebastian Carr was concerned. He was going to give the directives, and delegate the actual hard work which was necessary to bring in the much needed cash.

'Mr Pyke will see you before you leave, Miss Kepple.

Sister, see that all the arrangements are made for her to get home without stress, and lay on a car to bring her in to Outpatients two weeks from today.'

As they reached the corridor and Valda closed Miss Kepple's door Sebastian said, 'I see Miss Kepple likes strawberries too.'

Valda faced him confidently. 'We really couldn't eat any more, Mr Carr. Dad wanted me to bring them back with me so I thought of Miss Kepple. She has no relatives to visit her at all.'

He brushed her cheek with one finger. 'You're a very thoughtful, caring girl,' he said softly. 'I hope your staff and the rest of the patients don't see it as favouritism.'

'I've learnt how to be discreet. I doubt that anyone else noticed. Besides, no two patients are in identical situations. You, I think, made special dispensation to allay Miss Kepple's fears before her operation.'

Sebastian laughed spontaneously. 'Touché, Nordic beauty,' he whispered before they went into the next room.

When the round was finished and he had checked on patients who needed special treatments, and those he considered were ready for surgery, they drifted back to Valda's office where she offered him coffee which seemed the polite thing to do.

The invitation appeared to put him in some confusion and he gave the matter considerable thought before saying: 'Um . . . no thanks, I'd better get on as I'm meeting someone.'

Valda took a few steps beside him towards the door, and the next instant she watched him disappear round the corner and heard his echoing footsteps making for the stairs.

His touch had been no more than a flutter on her elbow, but it had set her whole body trembling. For several minutes she remained in the doorway of her office trying to retain that lightning brush which had caught her off guard. Only when she heard his footsteps disappear did she seem to gain enough impetus to turn back to her desk. Even then her brain refused to function. It was caught up in a whirl of perplexity.

The memory of the accidental meeting with him at Home Farm was never far from her mind. Not so accidental, she thought with a secret smile; a contrived one planned expertly by her father. That thought prompted her to phone him, advising him that he could only have Carlos for another two days.

'How would it be if I came in so that you can introduce us, official-like, then I can see that Miss Kepple's safely back in her own domain with Carlos,' her father suggested.

Valda agreed that this was a good idea. Afterwards she wondered whether she was in danger of becoming too familiar with a patient, but if Miss Kepple had had relatives or friends of her own they would be doing exactly as her father had suggested, and she knew that Miss Kepple would be delighted to see her dog again. She sat idly twisting the telephone cord between her fingers. She hoped Miss Kepple wouldn't read too much into her father's friendly manner. He was like that with everyone. He'd been a successful policeman because he tried to befriend those with whom he came into contact, victim and criminal alike. That, he maintained, was how to get the best out of people and he loved people. She wasn't surprised that he liked Sebastian Carr. In some ways they were two of a kind, but she wondered just what tales her father was telling about her.

CHAPTER FIVE

VALDA's thoughts were interrupted by a telephone call advising her of a new admission, and when a few moments later she went to the lift Tom, one of the porters, emerged pushing a disgruntled looking young man in a wheelchair.

'Hallo,' Valda greeted the patient cheerfully. 'Looks as if you've been in a fight.'

His clothes were bloodstained, his hands bandaged as well as a large pad over his right eye. He glanced disinterestedly at Valda and then down at his feet, his bruised lips firmly together with an expression of 'you won't get anything out of me'.

Tom passed Valda his notes.

'Room ten, Tom please,' Valda said as she led the way, reading as she went. She learnt that Lee Abbott was due in theatre first thing in the morning to have any glass removed and the cornea stitched.

Tom helped Lee on to the chair in the small one-bedded room, then left.

'Right, Lee,' Valda said. 'I expect you'll be glad of some rest. If you'd like to undress I'll go to find you some pyjamas.'

'Do I have to?' he grunted.

'I'm afraid you can't go to bed with your clothes on, and it looks as if they need laundering.'

She went away and was at the linen cupboard searching for a suitable pair of pyjamas when the night staff arrived on duty.

'I'll be with you in a minute,' she called to Pam Gardner. 'A new admission in number ten.'

'The first of many by the sound of things,' Pam said

with dismay. The main hospital Casualty is full of youths in black leather gear; broken noses and jaws, missing teeth, black eyes, you name it, they've got it.'

'Let's hope they don't send too many over here. This one is the unco-operative kind.'

Pam went on into the office and Valda returned to room ten.

Lee was still sitting in the chair as Valda had left him, but instead of wearing his shirt he was holding it in his hands surveying the damage.

She put the pyjamas by his side. 'Let's have those soiled clothes,' she ordered, 'then when you're in bed I'll take some particulars. They cleaned you up in Casualty, I see. Where can we send to get your belongings and a clean set of clothes?' she asked.

'Nowhere. All I possess was on my motor-cycle and it's all smashed up; I live rough, so I don't run to underwear and things like soap and towels.'

This admission surprised Valda. There was something pathetic about the young man and she felt some compassion for him. She made a bundle of his clothes and tied a label bearing his name and the ward on it and put it out on top of the laundry basket.

Valda knew from the notes that his eye had been badly gashed with glass, so time would tell whether or not the sight in that eye was impaired, or whether more severe damage might mean he would have to lose the eye altogether.

When she had signed off duty and reached her room Valda still kept thinking about Lee, but she'd been expecting a call from Adrian all day and it hadn't come so surely he must ring tonight? She guessed he would be at the club as she was familiar with his duty rota at the practice, and knew that he had not had an evening surgery, nor was he on call, but the minutes ticked by and at ten o'clock she went along to the kitchen to make herself a cup of hot chocolate.

She was surprised at how the time had flown by—it

was too late for Adrian to telephone now. When Valda had to be on duty at seven-thirty in the morning she liked to be in bed by ten-thirty the previous night, except on special occasions. Tomorrow, she thought hopefully as she sipped her bedtime drink, there was always tomorrow. Then she remembered that she was expected to go to the meeting the following evening. She had no excuse as she was due to finish work at four-thirty and so far had made no plans. Merle would of course be coming to the meeting to assist Sebastian Carr. Valda guessed that Adrian would phone and expect her to be available because Merle wouldn't be. Valda was well aware of her own obstinacy and now she vowed that she would go to Sebastian's meeting and to hell with Adrian Wallace. She knew she ought to feel ashamed at thinking such thoughts, but the truth was she didn't. However much she tried to convince herself that she would rather be with Adrian she was forced to admit that she was intrigued by the new consultant and his crusade, and in spite of herself, wanted to be a part of it. So Merle was his right-hand secretary, even that didn't put Valda off. She remembered that he had said he wouldn't have coffee on the ward as he was meeting someone—Merle—who else? So where and what was Adrian doing? She ought to have been bothered by his silence but she simply went to bed and fell asleep almost at once.

The next morning passed in the usual whirl of activity. One or two patients were going home after being discharged by Mr Carr the previous day. So many people came from outlying areas or remote villages among the Cotswold hills that it wasn't always possible to contact relatives or arrange transport to take them home until the following day.

Ray Pyke did a round with his houseman, and after visiting Lee Abbott who seemed quiet after his operation

Ray paced up and down Valda's office.

'It'll be a few days before we can assess the damage and whether or not he'll lose his sight or need to have the eye removed altogether,' he said with genuine disappointment.

'And only nineteen—it's so tragic. If only these boys would realise the dangers of getting into brawls,' Valda bemoaned.

'One of the other lads is in a critical condition in Intensive Care. He was stabbed several times. Most of them were able to go home after treatment, but one or two were kept in. Rival gangs met up by accident it seems, but Lee Abbott doesn't appear to have belonged to either. You'll get a visit from the police today of course.'

'I hope Lee will be more co-operative with them than he has been with us. Can't get much out of him at present but he has a rebellious attitude.'

'I doubt if he feels particularly rebellious this morning. The slit in the eyelid is bad enough. It's swollen and must be hellishly painful. Do the best you can to make him comfortable, Val. Mr Carr will see him tomorrow.'

'Perhaps it would be kinder to delay introducing him to the social worker for a day or two,' Valda suggested. 'We'll give him time to come round as he'll have enough on his plate today, what with feeling the after-effects of his injuries and getting a visit from the police.'

'I don't know why you should feel the necessity to be kind,' Ray said dispassionately. 'I'd put all these troublemakers on a remote Scottish island and let them suffer a few hardships with no means of returning to civilisation until they'd reformed.'

'Don't be such an old grumps,' Valda retorted. 'You were young once, and no angel, I bet.'

He turned and grinned at her. 'I consider I'm still young,' he said, 'but I didn't have much opportunity to rebel. All my time was taken up studying.'

'Young doctors in training have a certain reputation,'

Valda reminded him.

'Only of making passes at pretty nurses.' He leaned across her desk with a mischievous glint in his eye, but at that moment a young nurse arrived with a tray of coffee. 'Ah, that smells good, much better than the canteen stuff.'

'You realise how I spoil you,' Valda said. 'We're not supposed to do this, you know. These niceties are a thing of the past.'

'But you're a nice old-fashioned girl who likes to treat us all the same—and talking of our eminent consultant . . .'

'*Who* was talking about him?'

'*You* spoil him—consultants have to be pampered, so I bet you'll be the first one at his meeting tonight.'

Valda sighed. 'I suppose I ought to go out of a sense of duty. The equipment is for our department, after all.'

'Only a sense of duty?' Ray Pyke tut-tutted sarcastically. 'The rest of the staff are falling over themselves to be just where Sebastian is. I don't know whether it's his name, or what he's got that all the girls rave about.'

Valda didn't answer, but poured the coffee. Before Ray could drink half of his though his bleeper had summoned him to another part of the hospital and Valda settled down to reduce the amount of paperwork on her desk.

She was proud of being a ward Sister, but she missed the constant involvement with the patients and their needs. So much of her work now resulted in spending hours at her desk. Dressings, injections and medication were delegated to her team of staff nurses, second-and third-year pupil nurses while the more junior staff did the less responsible, though still necessary, tasks.

Despite the many interruptions she found that being alone at her desk gave her time to think, and some hours later she was still smarting over the fact that Ray had suggested that the entire female nursing staff were bent on being in Sebastian Carr's company. He probably wouldn't even notice whether she was present or not, and she mentally argued with herself as to whether she would go or whether she would put pride in her pocket and contact Adrian.

The main ward seemed reasonably free from any commotion when she finally visited the patients who occupied the beds in cubicles of four. Many of those who could get up were in the communal day-room which was a hubbub of chatter with the anticipation of visitors, and just as Valda was preparing to leave a young constable arrived to see Lee.

'Someone to see you, Lee,' Valda said cheerfully, but Lee lay motionless, pale, forlorn yet not the least perturbed at the sight of the policeman.

Valda finally went off duty, having suggested to her staff nurse that a cup of tea might ease the situation in room ten. So far she knew little of the fracas Lee had been involved in, but she desperately hoped that he hadn't done anything for which he could be prosecuted.

She walked slowly and thoughtfully across the grounds to Conifer Lodge. Still no word from Adrian, and although he had never had cause to write to her she found herself looking in the mail box, but there was nothing. She remembered that no mention had been made of when or where they would see each other again. Was this the end? Was Adrian waiting, expecting her to make the first move? Valda had to acknowledge that before Sebastian Carr had come to Addlefield she would have been desperate just to hear Adrian's voice by now, so Adrian would be flattering himself that Valda would make the running. This time she would play hard to get instead. Sebastian had said he was counting on her so she felt she owed the consultant that much, to at least go to hear what his crusade involved.

After she had been to the Sisters' lounge for tea she phoned her father to finalise the arrangements for him to come in to Addlefield to fetch Miss Kepple the following day. Then she went up to her room. She showered and washed her hair and while it was drying naturally she tried to decide what to wear. The warm weather was continuing so she selected a cotton jumpsuit in a rich ruby shade. It was elasticated at the waist and under-arm top, with tie-tapes on both shoulders. Light and cool, she had made this particular style because of the looseness of the bodice which helped to disguise her full bust. She loved sewing and was a competent needle-woman even to adapting patterns to make the garment exclusive to her. She had made a lightweight oatmeal coloured jacket with facings of the same ruby material to wear over the top.

She decided to wear high-heeled sandals in a neutral shade so was glad of enough time to re-varnish her toe-nails in a toning ruby colour. She did her finger-nails to match, though had to admit that it was a somewhat wasted effort as it would have to be removed before she went on duty again. The necklace and bangle she wore were of cheap red glass, but they matched well, and when she was ready, her silky blonde hair caught back in a red velvet ribbon, at least it gave her the feeling of being dressed for a social event.

She surveyed herself in the long mirror inside her wardrobe. Who had she dressed to please this evening? Was she desperately hoping that at the eleventh hour Adrian would phone and come to pick her up and whisk her away to a secluded spot where he would discover that all she was wearing underneath the jumpsuit was a tiny pair of briefs? Or was she out to impress Sebastian Carr?   She hadn't set out to make a spectacle of herself, and she did her best to enter the lecture hall alone and find a seat at the back of the room, but some of her colleagues reached the door at the same time and at once Valda was the centre of attention. She was well known for her unique choice of clothes, envied for her lustrous blonde hair, and now they complimented and wanted to see her outfit in detail.

One of the young housemen from Sebastian's team was on the door. 'Are you girls having a gossip session out there or are you coming in to the meeting?' he whispered as Sebastian Carr's voice echoed from the platform.

Valda stood back and let her friends go in first, and to her dismay as she was ushered in she saw that the hall was crowded. She didn't glance towards the speaker, but knew that he had paused while the houseman indicated one of two vacant chairs at the end of a row about half way down. As soon as he started to speak again Valda looked up and with a pang of discomfort saw Merle sitting beside Sebastian. The chair on his other side was vacant.

'This is an informal meeting,' Sebastian said, 'and I would like the entire scheme to be viewed as a fun thing. To make a fund-raising appeal work we must all be seen to be enjoying what we're doing, and at the same time be sincere in our cause.'

He went on to explain the great benefits which the laser machine would provide for patients, especially diabetics whose condition affected every system in the body. The powerful light of the laser would be able to obliterate fragile vessels in the eye which otherwise would break and cause a haemorrhage. He mentioned factual cases where laser treatment had been effective and quick. That he was a competent speaker as well as dedicated and enthusiastic in his profession was evident, and everyone appeared to be mesmerised by his oration. Finally he invited questions, and after one or two someone mentioned forming a committee.

Sebastian smiled and smoothed his square chin with a deliberate look of mortification. 'I trust you will all forgive me, but as there is a certain amount of urgency in raising the money—the longer we owe the bank for the machine the more expensive it will be—I've taken it upon myself to act as Chairman and I've already appointed a few helpers.'

It was at this point that a few whisperings echoed round the room, but Valda noticed that both Sebastian and Merle's attention was riveted to the rear of the hall.

Sebastian went on: 'I'm glad to say some people have come forward voluntarily which has pleased me immensely, namely my worthy secretary here, Merle Decarta who has had several years' experience as a medical secretary.'

At that moment Valda felt someone at her side, and looking to her left discovered Adrian sliding as noiselessly as he could into the seat beside her.

Adrian's gaze was full of admiration and Valda's doubts faded instantly as he took her hand and squeezed it affectionately. She suddenly felt she had everything in the world which was good. She wanted to demonstrate her feelings, tell him how much she had missed him, but this was not the place for such intimate conversation. Instead their eyes held sweet communion, and only when the now distant voice of Sebastian Carr mentioned Valda's name, at which everyone laughed, did she come back to the meeting.

Sebastian was looking with directness at her. What had he said? Was he waiting for her to say something? Had he asked her a question personally? There were titters all around the room and Valda held on to Adrian's hand for reassurance.

'Evidently Miss Bergman left us briefly, so I'll repeat that I've delegated some of the organisation to her.'

Valda went tight inside. How dare he make such an assumption and exhibition of her! She hadn't agreed to do anything.

With a captivating smile Sebastian continued: 'Merle here will do all the paperwork, and Valda will see that every member of the staff has a sponsorship form. It is then up to the individual to get friends, relatives, even patients, to sponsor you in whichever event you decide to compete.'

To the last detail Sebastian Carr had organised everything, he just needed to delegate the hard work to
others, and inveigle everyone into taking part, and the
list was endless. Sponsored swims, sponsored walks,
dances, raffles, some of which had already started with
crocheted blankets, cuddly toys, and paintings by local
artists on display at the Addlefield Health Centre. The
local Army base were setting up an assault course, and
the event to which everyone would be pressured into
taking part was a five-mile race, a circular route having
been devised starting and ending at the hospital.

A few light-hearted questions ended the session. No
one dared argue against the consultant on any point,
and everyone readily agreed to his small committee
which consisted of Danny Banks as Vice-Chairman,
Ray Pyke as Treasurer, Merle his secretary and the
Outpatients Sister, Liz Bath, a committee member along
with Valda.

'King's Jester for a drink?' Adrian whispered as
everyone began to move.

'Oh—yes—please,' Valda breathed, anxious to get
away from the crowded hall.

It was gone ten o'clock so almost dark but a beautiful
moonlit night as, with arms entwined, Adrian and Valda
walked along the country lane which led to the inn.

'The outfit looks stunning,' Adrian said, in between
long, passionate kisses to which Valda eagerly responded,
and as soon as they reached the King's Jester she found
a secluded corner alcove while Adrian fetched the drinks.
The pub had obviously been busy, but now people were
thinning out; all the same it was very warm so Valda
slipped off her jacket. When Adrian returned with the
drinks he was appreciative of her bare shoulders and
the soft feel of her body through the fine material.

Any minute he would say 'let's go for a drive', but
he seemed content to talk about the meeting, and all
that the appeal involved, while Valda was only aware

of his gentle fingertips caressing sensitive parts of her body, driving her into a state of elevation. But her spirits fell flat when the door opened and some of the staff entered, among them Merle and Sebastian accompanied by Liz Bath, Ray and Danny.

'Keep quiet and no one will notice us,' Valda whispered.

Adrian looked at her quickly, then laughed. 'How can I hide such a gorgeous creature as you, especially with that give-away hair?'

Valda watched closely as Merle remained attached to Sebastian's side, but suddenly she turned and it was as if she knew exactly where to find Adrian. She walked across the carpeted floor, dodging between tables and chairs until she reached them.

'Come on, Jack's reserved a long table for all of us over there; let's all be together.'

Adrian stood up and immediately followed Merle, leaving Valda to straggle on behind them, fury bubbling up inside. She stopped to shrug her shoulders into her jacket as she tried to cope with her bag in one hand, her drink in the other.

More of the staff had arrived by now so the long table was rapidly filling up. Adrian was sitting opposite Merle, but he managed to pat the seat beside him as Valda placed her drink down on the table, and in so doing her jacket slid to the floor. She turned to pick it up and almost bumped heads with Sebastian who had retrieved it.

'This is being a nuisance,' he said, 'I'll hang it up,' and before Valda could protest he had taken it to some wall pegs and hung it up.

He came back to sit next to Merle, facing Valda.

'Well, what did you think of the meeting?' he asked her.

Valda took a sizeable sip of her sweet sherry to steady her frayed nerves. 'Fine,' she said, but *she* felt anything but fine. The noise, laughter and banter went on around her. She answered vaguely when she was spoken to, but was thankful that the men were more concerned with quenching their thirst and in the dim lighting of the pub she could sit quietly and wallow in her misery. She was disappointed that she and Adrian hadn't gone off somewhere together, but in her loneliness she recognised the fact that this furtherance of the meeting had been planned. By Merle and Adrian if no one else.

'I'll let you have the sponsorship forms, Valda,' Merle said loudly, doing her best to include Valda. 'I can pop them up to your ward, or Adrian can deliver them.'

'Yes . . . yes, thanks,' Valda muttered, and every time she was obliged to answer she rushed to take another sip of her drink. Soon it would be gone; it was disappearing so rapidly that she began to feel dizzy. She wished it had a magical way of turning her into a vivacious, bubbly extrovert like Merle, but instead of cheering up she was becoming more downcast.

'Pity you can't swim,' Merle said, 'but Adrian says you're a good sportswoman otherwise. There's the assault course, and the big race.'

'You should do well in that,' Sebastian said. 'Not that winning is important, but finishing so that your sponsors have to pay up.'

'We shall all need to jog and get plenty of exercise so that we're fit,' Danny said. 'We can make it a group thing, and with this new club in town there'll be no excuse for anyone.'

Valda felt like saying that she, like most nurses, got enough exercise on the wards without doing any extra, but everyone else seemed so enthusiastic about the fund-raising that she felt the odd one out. She drained her schooner and Adrian raised his eyebrows as he picked up her empty glass.

'What's the matter with you tonight?' he teased. 'Usually one drink lasts you all evening. Want another?'

'No thanks.' She had almost added that she must be going soon when a shadow fell across the end of the

table and a bright female voice greeted: 'Oh, there you
are! Darling, I've been looking everywhere for you.'

Valda knew at once that the voice was familiar, and
who else but Miranda would be holding a dog's lead?

Sebastian stood up and pecked Miranda's cheek
lightly.

'It's almost closing time. Would you like a drink?' he
asked.

Miranda shook her jet black hair. 'No thanks, I'm
driving, but I thought I'd look you up before I go home
so that you can see Misty is being properly looked
after.'

Misty was the enormous Great Dane at the end of
the lead. He was a superb creature with a dark grey
velvety coat, and he seemed mesmerised by Valda.
Although she was fond of dogs she didn't feel too
confident about this large animal whose face, even when
sitting as commanded, was level with hers.

Everyone chorused that he'd taken a shine to Valda
but she would have felt happier if he had shown his
loyalty to his master. Adrian leaned across in front of
Valda to make a fuss of Misty who responded excitably
by promptly putting his two front paws on Valda's
knees. He licked her face and neck much to everyone's
amusement.

'Control him, Miranda!' Sebastian's voice was sharp,
tinged with impatient anger.

Valda did her best to recover from hiding her face
behind Adrian's back. She remembered how much she
had liked Miranda, the young kennelmaid with glossy
black hair and white flawless skin. Valda noticed that
she too was wearing a jumpsuit but it was made of soft
velour in midnight blue, and wasn't as revealing as her
own. She hadn't known that Miranda and Sebastian
were friends and wouldn't have admitted to anyone that
this fact struck the final blow to her already wounded
pride.

Sebastian stood up, took the lead from Miranda and

led Misty outside with Miranda following. Merle got up too, saying that she must get home, and soon everyone else followed suit.

Adrian helped Valda on with her jacket, and as they went out again into the balmy summer night the topic of conversation centred around Sebastian's dog. The others were strolling down the lane towards the hospital, Adrian and Valda in slow pursuit, and when they came to a farm gate Adrian drew Valda off the road. He held her close and kissed her ardently.

'Can't let Misty get away with all the fun,' he joked as he slid his hands beneath her jacket, spanning her trim waist. She couldn't resist his smooth, persuasive lips even though at the back of her mind she was sure Merle was waiting for him, but as they resumed the walk down the lane a white sports car came towards them from the hospital. The driver hooted the discordant sounding horn and Valda recognised that it was Merle behind the wheel.

'Super car,' Valda commented when the roar of its engine had died away in the distance.

Adrian sighed. 'Daughter of the idle rich. "Daddy" changes her car every year for her, so she says.'

'Does she live with her parents?'

'Heavens, no. She's in the flat next to mine—that's how I got mine. Her family are London business people. Something in the City, don't you know.' Adrian laughed at his own mimicry and pulled Valda closer to him with a playful squeeze.

In wriggling away from him she noticed a moving shadow behind them. She caught Adrian's hand to prevent him teasing. 'Behave,' she said. 'Someone's coming behind us.'

'So?'

'It could be one of your patients,' she said in mock reproach.

He pulled her arm through his and they walked happily into the hospital car-park. When they reached his car Adrian unlocked his door. 'In the back?' he suggested with a grin.

'It's too late, darling,' Valda said.

He hugged her close. 'A good night's sleep always follows the best exercise in the world.'

'Not in the car-park,' she whispered.

His hands roamed over her thinly clad figure. Her heart was beating in expectation and then he kissed her mouth decisively.

'See you at the weekend perhaps, though I shall be on call,' he said as he moved her away from the door, and in a matter of minutes he'd started up the engine and was gone. After all the let downs of the day this was just one more. She felt restless, and knew that she wouldn't go to sleep even if she went to bed. Lights were going on and off all over the hospital. She was in the car-park which lay between the old and new hospitals and gazing back towards the old hospital, now the Ear, Nose, Throat and Eye Unit, she suddenly wondered how Lee was. He seemed so alone in the world with no visitors except a policeman, but it really was too late to go visiting now. There were few cars left, mostly night staff's, and Valda walked across the open space feeling that it was an eerie, sinister place to be alone and midnight approaching.

From somewhere she heard her name called. She turned, expecting to see someone coming in the direction of the hospital. She had intended to go through the rear of the hospital grounds and enter Conifer Lodge through the garden, but now as she tried to control her agitation she pushed her way between shrubs to the road and came face to face with Sebastian.

'You made me jump,' she said in a croaky, frightened voice. 'I didn't expect to meet anyone else.'

'What are you doing here anyway?' he asked sternly. 'Doesn't Adrian see you to the door?'

Valda shrugged, annoyed that he was so ready to accuse Adrian of thoughtlessness.

'I'm home,' she said lamely. 'He has to go to the other side of Addlefield.'

'That's no excuse. You never know who's lurking about in car-parks at this time of night.' He took her arm and escorted her to the entrance of Conifer Lodge.

'I was going to see Lee Abbott,' she said by way of making excuses, 'but it's too late.'

Sebastian swung her round and faced her fiercely in the moonlight. 'There are adequate night staff in every ward and on every department. You're getting carried away with devotion. You're off duty and you must learn to leave your work in the wards.'

'Not much chance of that,' Valda retorted indignantly, 'when all our waking hours from now on are going to be concerned with raising money for your appeal.'

'That's different, and you know it.' He gripped her arm tightly. 'I was disappointed in you tonight. Of course, it was good of you to give up your evening off to come to the meeting, but the chair on my right was meant for you. I'd hoped you and Merle were going to work together.'

'Don't I work hard enough as it is?' Valda snapped angrily. The very idea of working closely with Merle filled her with awe. 'I'm not keen on this idea of asking people to sponsor me to do something. Everyone does it, the children at school, every charity gets up sponsored walks and things.'

'Have you got any better ideas?'

Valda fell silent. She hadn't, and it annoyed her that she couldn't come up with something special, but just about everything had been done.

'Of course,' Sebastian said sarcastically, 'if you feel that you're too old to take part, I'll be grateful if you'll help in an administrative way, keep tabs on the forms. I don't want anyone to have too much to do, but if everyone helps in however small a way it'll bring us all closer together.'

Valda sighed. 'I don't like being pressurised,' she said.

'Then I'll have to resort to gentle persuasion,' he replied, his tone softer.

Valda turned to walk up the drive of Conifer Lodge.

'I'm quite all right now,' she said as he fell into step beside her, but he kept right there with her and inside the conservatory he grabbed her roughly.

'I could say you're being bloody-minded. You're very obstinate, Valda. Why? Is it that deep down you perhaps prefer to be pressurised?'

He took her in his arms, but just as she braced herself for the expected kiss he let her go abruptly, and with a curt 'Goodnight' was gone.

CHAPTER SIX

WAS it Miranda's charm, the memory of her kisses which had made Sebastian falter? Valda was confident that he had been going to kiss her. Whatever the mood, however much back-biting went on between them, they seemed to spontaneously end up poles apart, and now she experienced a sinking feeling of unparalleled depths. She sat on the side of her bed, her hands supporting her on either side behind her as she endeavoured to analyse her feelings. She thought she loved Adrian, but the truth was she couldn't or there would be no doubts. Oh, she liked him a lot. When he had first come to Addlefield he had been glad to find a diversion from work. That's all she had been to him. He accused her of wanting a serious relationship, but that was just what he didn't want. A bed-mate, yes, and a girl whom he could be proud to have at his side wherever he went. She knew she had all the physical qualities a man required, but deep down they didn't have the right feeling between them which would progress to a serious relationship. Her father had noticed that the vital ingredient was missing. By occasional remarks he made Valda knew that he thought their friendship was too casual to warrant planning a future together. He was right. If Valda found excuses for not giving in to Adrian's demands, Adrian always had a ready excuse for not being able to see her. She considered the friendships some of the other nurses and Sisters had. The telephone was always busiest between nine and ten at night. Often the girls would skip supper in order to dash off for just an hour with their loved one, but there never seemed that passionate urgency between Adrian

86

and herself. Any urgency, she reflected, had been on her part. She wanted to believe that Adrian felt the same way, but now she doubted that he cared for her enough to put her before all else. Besides, he'd developed an attraction for Merle, it seemed.

Valda traced her thoughts back to earlier this evening. Adrian had certainly surprised her by turning up at the meeting. She wondered why he hadn't phoned to tell her. It couldn't have been because he had come with Merle as she had been there early and Adrian had come in half-way through. Then she felt sick as she realised that if she hadn't been at the meeting she would never have known that Adrian had been there, so he and Merle could have gone off and done what she guessed they were doing now! How convenient to have flats next door to one another. She decided then and there that she would never go to Adrian's flat again.

She couldn't imagine life without him, they'd had some good times, but now too many of her secret thoughts went in another direction. No, she simply refused to admit that she loved Sebastian Carr. The very thought of such a thing made her cringe with self-condemnation. She must nip that in the bud before she found herself unable to control her emotion. He had Miranda, and a reputation by all accounts.

Valda's light burned on as the surroundings of the hospital and Sisters' home became enveloped in darkness. It was useless to think of sleep, she was too confused by all that had happened. Miranda and Sebastian? She was so young, no more than twenty, a girl who loved animals and the outdoor country life. It all went with the other image of Sebastian. He helped his sister Jessica with her farming, but he had said that he didn't live with her. Did he live with Miranda? Surely she didn't live alone in that splendid bungalow, but Sebastian hadn't accompanied her home tonight. He had appeared seemingly from nowhere.

Valda undressed and hung up her clothes, washed

her face and put a cotton nightdress on before sliding
between the sheets, her mind still a maze of confusion.
She stared into the darkness, wild imaginings keeping
her alert.

She felt heavy-lidded when she went on duty next
morning. Coffee and a piece of dry wholemeal toast
was all she managed to consume in the five minutes
available for breakfast after she had removed the varnish
from her finger-nails. She guessed she would be hungry
within an hour. Nursing was one job where you burnt
off calories faster than you could count them on a
normal working day, but even before she had listened
to the night report she knew there was no promise of
today being normal. Or, she thought with a touch of
irony, perhaps normal was trying to be in half a dozen
places at once.

An elderly gentleman was in great distress, the trauma
of being in hospital having precipitated an acute stage
in his prostate condition. Pam Gardner had sent out an
urgent call for a houseman to come to deal with the
patient, but as always there was some delay. Valda did
all she could to make him comfortable, though the
intense pain he was suffering resulted in cries of agony
until at last the houseman arrived.

The night staff were just leaving when Duncan Fraser,
the young newly qualified doctor, came into the office.

'Keep an eye on old Mr Stanford, please, Sister. This
sort of upset isn't good for his heart. At least he's out
of pain now, but his breathing is laboured. I think we
ought to get Mr Pyke to see him later.'

'Right,' Valda said, making a note on Mr Stanford's
folder. 'He'll be round before he goes into theatre.
We've quite a few local anaesthetics today, and one or
two discharges he'll have to see as well. You'll be round
again to see the new admissions?'

'I will that, if I haven't fallen by the wayside by

lunchtime,' he groaned.

'You've evidently been on call all night,' Valda said with a smile.

'How did you guess?' Duncan quipped. 'You too by the looks of things. These lucky fellas who can keep their girl-friends up until the early hours,' he tut-tutted as he went on his way.

Valda visited the patients on the theatre list first, most of whom were apprehensive, though it was usually other post-operative patients who were best at comforting the ones still waiting.

As she came to room ten she was surprised to hear lots of giggles and two junior nurses collided with her in the doorway.

'If you have nothing better to do,' Valda snapped, 'you can prepare room three for a mother and daughter, Nurse Rippon, and you, Nurse Dickson, check that Miss Kepple can manage; she's going home today.'

Both girls shot off, their frivolity ending flatly at the unusual reprimand from Valda, who went in to room ten to find Lee Abbott still in bed.

'Good morning, Lee. How are you this morning?' she asked, noticing that his face generally looked decidedly less marked than previously, and there was a mischievous twinkle in his good eye.

'Playing the bossy Sister are we today then, blondie?' Lee answered sarcastically. Valda gave him an icy glare at his familiarity.

'Nurses are here to work, Lee, we all are, not to play around with you.'

'You can play around with me any time, blondie.'

'I see,' Valda replied pointedly, 'you're evidently feeling better, so come on, up and dressed, I think.'

'You took my clothes—remember?'

'I'll soon chase them up. They'll be back from the laundry by now. Have you washed and shaved?'

'Yep,' he answered, 'but that doesn't mean I want to get up. I don't feel like it. I was just trying to catch one of those pretty birds to come and keep me company.'

'Up, and in the day room,' Valda retorted stonily.

Lee sat up, leaning forward to look directly at Valda from his good unpatched eye. 'Come and get me,' he goaded.

'We have strong male nurses and housemen for people like you,' she said, unimpressed. 'Mr Carr is coming to see you today and he likes his patients to show some enthusiasm. It's no good lying there feeling sorry for yourself.'

'Who says I'm feeling sorry for myself? I just want to get out of here,' he said.

'Isn't this better than sleeping rough?'

'No—not when there's always some busybody interfering.'

Valda wanted to ask if he'd told the policeman he was interfering, but at that moment she was called away to the telephone.

Without a doubt it was 'that' kind of day, she thought dismally after it had taken two telephone calls, and sparing a junior nurse to track down Lee Abbott's laundered clothes which, in spite of being clearly labelled, had been returned to men's surgical ward at the main hospital, by which time Ray Pyke had visited the unit and gone off to start his theatre list.

Although it was much later than usual to go for a mid-morning break, Valda had reached the corridor on the lower floor when she bumped into her father, accompanied by Sebastian Carr.

'Hallo, my dear,' Howard greeted, squeezing her arm gently.

'Morning, Sister,' Sebastian said lightly. 'I've just done something which you should have done months ago, and that is taken your father to the new hospital building and shown him over it.'

'I didn't think you'd be interested,' Valda said, giving her father a hesitant, quizzical look.

'I'm always interested in anything that concerns you,'

he said with an affectionate smile, 'but I know it's necessary to keep your family and profession apart.'

'The rules aren't that rigid,' Sebastian quipped, 'and if we want people to help us raise money we've got to encourage them to become familiar with the hospital and its workings. Had a good meeting last night, didn't we, Valda?' He was suddenly more personal.

'Yes,' she murmured quietly, then to her father: 'I was just going for coffee so you'd better come too.'

'You're too late,' Sebastian cut in smoothly, 'we've had ours. I'm here to see the young man in your charge so—instead of coffee, have an early lunch.' He took her arm and turned her round in that disarming but dominant way he had, his eyes full of mischief.

He was being a sight too familiar, Valda thought petulantly, and she felt like telling him to go on to room ten while she talked to her father, but one glance at him and she knew she was under his influence. And there was her father too, grinning like a Cheshire cat as if he'd engineered everything his way. He might think so, she thought angrily, but he doesn't know the half of it. Miranda was someone even the great Howard Bergman hadn't reckoned with.

'You're looking tired, Valda,' her father admonished gently as they went up in the lift. 'Do you feel all right?'

'Fine,' she answered more sharply than she intended. 'Oh,' she groaned by way of excusing her irritation, 'it's one of those days. I have a feeling that it's going to end badly.'

'If Miss Kepple can wait I could take you out to lunch,' Howard suggested kindly, and the grace with which he took her bad temper brought a lump to her throat. She was just being a bitch she scolded, and after a moment she composed herself and turned with a smile.

'Don't tempt me, Dad. It's a lovely idea, thanks all the same, but for one thing Miss Kepple is eager to see her little dog again, and I look like getting off at about two o'clock if I'm lucky.'

They reached the upper floor and Valda led the way to Miss Kepple's room, but they found it empty.

'In the day-room then probably,' Valda said, and as they moved along the passageway the swing doors at the end opened and Miss Kepple came through, helped by Lee Abbott.

'Oh, there you are. This is my father, Miss Kepple,' Valda began, but the look of astonishment on Lee Abbott's face stopped her from continuing.

'Sarge—Sarge Bergman,' Lee clicked his fingers. ' 'Course—Sister Bergman—blondie's *your* daughter?— I never thought—' Lee stopped, evidently thinking twice before he committed himself. Valda guessed he was going to say how could a starchy hospital sister be Howard's daughter, for there was clearly great admiration in his gaze directed at her father.

'Been in the wars, Lee?' Howard Bergman asked kindly.

'You could say so,' Lee answered, then jerked his head down at Miss Kepple. 'So you're the godfather that took in Miss Kepple's dog?—well, she'd better go, she can't wait to see that you've been feeding him properly.'

'Oh, go on with you, Lee,' Miss Kepple admonished good-naturedly. 'Now you take care, my boy, I shall be anxious to know how things go for you, but you couldn't be in better hands than Sister here, and Mr Carr.'

Lee actually smiled and gave Miss Kepple a gentle tap on her shoulder as he turned to go.

'I'll be back to see you, Lee,' Howard Bergman called after him cheerfully, and Valda led the way to her office.

Valda couldn't help noticing that Miss Kepple had washed her hair and even sported a little extra make-up especially for her father's benefit. She was pale and a little shaky still, but very determined and naturally anxious to see Carlos.

When the formalities had been dealt with and Valda had given her an appointment card to visit Mr Carr's clinic in two weeks' time, she took Valda's hand and held it firmly.

'My dear, you've been so kind, I can't thank you enough. Now, when you all get your sponsorship forms for whatever part you're going to play I want you to put my name on it.'

Valda laughed awkwardly. 'I'm only handling the forms, Miss Kepple,' she said.

'You're going to do more than that, young lady. It's up to you to set an example to the rest of the staff,' Sebastian intervened. 'I'm going to compete with you in the assault course the local Army are arranging for us.'

'Oh no!' Valda cried. 'I couldn't possibly.'

Howard Bergman laughed. 'Miss Kepple, I think we'll be on our way—looks like there's going to be a fight.'

For the next moment or two the laser appeal was forgotten as Howard, carrying Miss Kepple's few belongings, escorted her to the lift where Valda wished her well and said goodbye.

Valda hurried back to her office where Sebastian was in the place he so often favoured, at the window surveying the landscape once more bathed in sunshine.

'Mr Carr,' she began decisively. 'Once and for all *I'll* decide what help I can give to the appeal. I simply refuse to beg money from pensioners and patients who are in a vulnerable state after treatment and surgery. It's all right among friends, but it's up to each individual to do the best they can within their own limits.'

She suddenly recognised her own voice, arrogant, high-pitched, and she was obliged to pause for breath while she toyed with papers on her desk.

'Would you care to see Lee Abbott now?' Her tone was similar to that which she used to the junior nurses when something went wrong.

Sebastian turned slowly and sat on the window-sill

watching her with hooded intuitive eyes. Her temper cooled. She had gone too far. Now what?

'Yes, I'll see Lee Abbott in my consulting room shortly. If I didn't know differently, Valda, I might think you're resentful of my efforts to have the best equipment for our patients' benefit. Or is it that you think fund-raising is going to come between you and Adrian? I must say he has been most co-operative. I hoped we would all enter into the spirit of the project as a team, and disprove the fallacy that work and play don't mix.'

'In this profession work and play *can't* mix,' she said positively.

Sebastian looked at her with a triumphant gleam in his eyes. 'You seem to have formed a rather familiar relationship with this young man, Lee Abbott,' he rebuked mildly. 'I must say I'm surprised at you. By all accounts he's of questionable character. You can't befriend every lame duck who turns up on your ward, you know. Helping a lonely spinster like Miss Kepple is one thing, making friends with a layabout is another.'

Valda was almost spitting sparks. How could he condemn when he had not even met Lee Abbott, and whatever made him think that she had befriended the lad?

'As far as Lee Abbott is concerned I've done no more than I do for any of my patients, and I'm shocked to hear you criticise a patient when as yet you haven't met him. We're here in a professional capacity, Mr Carr. It isn't our job to discriminate between patients. I'm only interested in making sick people well—and—' she added, her eyes bright with anger, 'I'm glad my father taught me to believe that there is some good in everyone. It's just harder to find in some people,' she finished pointedly.

Sebastian had started to walk towards her. His eyes were stinging in their intensity but after a hesitant glance towards the open door he spoke softly but distinctly.

'We'll continue this discussion another time, Sister, but why not try to find the good in me instead of always fighting me?'

He stalked off to the consulting room with an impatient nod indicating that he was ready to examine Lee. Valda's head felt as if it would burst. She'd actually shouted at a consultant, but he'd managed to create havoc in the short time he'd been at Addlefield. So the hospital needed a laser machine. Didn't she know that better than anyone? Why must he make it sound as if she alone had to raise the money? She clenched her fists. This was indeed a bad day and she regretted that her father had witnessed her peevishness. Worst of all was Sebastian's insinuation that she wasn't in favour of being part of the team which would work towards getting the much needed laser machine. She moved things on her desk, doing nothing in particular when the telephone bell made her start. She picked up the receiver and even before she could speak Sebastian's curt voice echoed sharply: 'I'm waiting, Sister.'

She knew by his tone of voice and the sharp clatter as he replaced the receiver that he was displeased with her. Somehow she had to restrain her irritation, but it wasn't easy. She picked up Lee's folder of notes and walked as sedately as she could to room ten. It would just be her luck if Lee had gone to the day-room, and to her dismay she found his room empty. She hurried along the extended corridor to the day room but there was no sign of him, neither was he in any of the wards. Then Valda heard female laughter coming from the bathroom and shower area.

Valda didn't mean to creep in on them; it was just that they were so engrossed in each other that they didn't hear her approach.

'Lee, Mr Carr is waiting to see you now,' she said sharply.

'Sister—' began Nurse Rippon, flushed with embarrassment.

'Hurry up, Lee,' Valda said, ignoring the younger girl, 'consultants don't like to be kept waiting,' and she started to walk away, hoping that Lee was following. She half-turned and saw that he was looking somewhat dishevelled already in his freshly laundered clothes. At least his jeans were clean, Valda thought, and his checked shirt had been washed and patched, but she didn't like the way he was wearing it outside his jeans. He seemed to be walking awkwardly too, and Valda went hot and cold in turn as she guessed what she might have broken up between him and Nurse Rippon. She'd have to be on her guard from now on but she hoped it wouldn't mean the young nurse having to be moved as she was a good worker. She also had a happy disposition which endeared her to the patients.

At last they reached the door of the consulting room after tramping silently through what seemed endless corridors. It was half-open so Valda knocked lightly and walked straight in.

Sebastian was sitting at his desk and didn't even look up as Valda placed Lee's notes on the corner of the desk.

Just the sight of his long slender fingers brought a look of admiration to her eyes, but it was quickly suppressed as he muttered: 'What kept you?'

'I'm sorry, sir, I couldn't find Lee.'

Valda indicated to Lee that he should sit down opposite the consultant. She removed the bandage and pad over his eye and put it in the bin.

At length Sebastian slowly lifted his eyes to Valda and his look was a mixture of smouldering contempt and annoyance.

'You look as if you need that coffee,' he remarked coldly. 'I shall be some time with Lee. I shan't require your help.'

Valda turned and left the room, closing the door decisively behind her. She felt snubbed; doctors of whatever grade expected to have a nurse in attendance.

So this man was different—yes, he was certainly that, she conceded. She went straight to the kitchen and made herself some strong black coffee, then she took it to her office and sat down staring at the telephone. It would ring. Any minute Sebastian would summon her assistance, but the inanimate plastic object remained dead.

By now her head was throbbing violently so she took a couple of aspirins and her staff nurse came in to discuss the afternoon's work with her.

'You look as if you need a little lie down, Sister,' she suggested lightly.

Valda managed a weak smile. 'That's the best sugges-tion I've heard today.' She glanced out of the window. 'This lovely weather ought to make me feel energetic, but it doesn't.'

'Can't you have a lie in the sun somewhere?'

'Mm, I might do. I keep promising myself a trip into town, there are a few nice shops up at the end where the new one-way system is.'

'Yes, Addlefield is looking up, especially with our new Sports Centre. Have you joined?'

Valda shook her head. 'I'm not that addicted to sport. The annual subscription is pretty steep so you need plenty of spare time to reap the benefits.'

'And we all know what we're expected to be doing in our spare time. You'll soon be chasing us up with fund-raising forms, I suppose?'

'Oh, don't.' Valda held her head in her hands. 'I just don't want to think of things like that today. I'm going off duty a bit early to see if I can shake off this thumping head. I'll leave you to be on hand if Mr Carr requires any assistance. I'm due back at five so Mr Pyke should have finished in the theatre by then unless Casualty send any across. Let's hope I feel better able to cope by then, and—um—there's the little girl and her Mum to go in room three. She's for theatre tomorrow and there are five more to come in for the main wards, one of whom is a diabetic.'

Valda still sat on trying not to will the telephone to ring or to make it obvious that she was listening for the sound of footsteps. She did so want to be around when Sebastian finished his examination of Lee so that she could hear his verdict first hand, but with every minute which passed her head drummed the more and it became evident that Staff Nurse Adey was wondering why Valda didn't just go. Eventually it was with some reluctance that she left the unit. Her feet and legs felt heavy as she crossed the back of the old hospital building to the garden, and although a lounger chair in the sunshine appealed to her she knew it would do her headache little good.

Remembering her scant breakfast and no mid-morning break she wondered if hunger was the cause of her feeling wretched, but the thought of food only made her feel worse so she took off her clothes, drew the curtains and slipped into bed thankfully. She refused to admit that these attacks were migraine even though she knew that her mother had been a sufferer all her adult life. Her father insisted that she didn't get enough fresh air and he was probably right, she thought.

She wondered how her father and Miss Kepple were getting on. Their meeting hadn't been the way Valda had planned. She hadn't even made a good job of introducing them with Sebastian Carr present and Lee escorting Miss Kepple. Now Lee couldn't be all bad, she thought, remembering his interest in Carlos and the affectionate way he had patted Miss Kepple on her shoulder. Valda hadn't much time to dwell on the surprising fact that Lee and her father seemed well acquainted. She snuggled deeper into the bed. Her father, bless him, knew everyone for miles around. That was all part of a policeman's job. It did rather point to the fact that Lee might have a record—still—that was no reason not to feel some compassion in the certain knowledge that he was about to lose his eye. No one, however bad, deserved that at nineteen.

Gradually noises from outside began to recede and with them her thoughts which held the key to the tension which had caused her to feel less than her usual lively self.

She slept for only an hour or so, but it was a good revitalising sleep and afterwards she soaked in a warm bath before covering her skin with sun oil and then, like some of her colleagues, she emerged into the garden wearing a brief blue and white bikini. The Sisters were lucky to have such a well laid-out and maintained garden. The conservatory at the side of the old house was large enough for several people to sit comfortably and some of the older women preferred it there to the garden. There was a paved patio outside the lounge where tea was being served, and beyond a huge velvety lawn surrounded by shrubs which secured privacy.

Valda poured herself a cup of tea and realised when she saw the bread, butter, jam, and rock cakes how hungry she was. She carried her tray to a corner of the lawn where she spread out a towel, and after she had eaten she protected her eyes with sun-glasses and stretched out in the hope of improving the colour of her skin. She didn't have long to indulge herself, but half an hour front and back should prove beneficial, and when she eventually returned to duty she felt more relaxed in every way.

Her staff nurse reported to her immediately. 'No sign of the little girl and her mother, but the last of the five adults is just being admitted now. We've had a busy afternoon with all the post-operative cases, but Mr Pyke has finished and will be around with the houseman later on.'

'And the good or bad news concerning Lee Abbott?' Valda asked.

'Ah—now—yes—' Staff Nurse Adey looked crestfallen. 'The worst I'm afraid. Mr Carr was with him for a good hour after you'd left, then he came out looking

for you. Lee was obviously pretty shattered and Mr
Carr went with him to his room and stayed for quite a
while. By this time Lee had missed lunch so Mr Carr
went to the canteen and fetched a tray for them both,
even though I offered to go and get Lee's.' Valda raised
her eyebrows then recalled that earlier she had decided
Sebastian Carr was different, and he was living up to
his reputation in more ways than one.

'He's having the little girl, Caroline, in theatre first
tomorrow, then Lee.'

Staff Nurse Adey went on to give the details about
the new admissions and post-operative cases and they
worked together until the staff nurse went off duty at
six o'clock.

Valda visited all the patients and at last the wards
seemed to be settling down to a quieter routine. She left
Lee until last. She desperately wanted to see him, yet
what was there for her to say? How had he taken the
news that he would have to wear a glass eye for the rest
of his life?

The door of room ten was tightly closed so she gave
a perfunctory knock and went in.

'Hallo, Lee—how's tricks?' she greeted brightly
without sounding too nonchalant. She saw instantly
how pale he was as he stood by the bed. Valda guessed
that he might have been pacing up and down the small
room ever since the consultant had left him.

'Hallo, blondie.' It was a valiant effort to be brave.
'And before you start commiserating, I'm lucky to be
losing only one eye.'

'Lee,' Valda's voice with just a hint of reproach belied
the absolute despair she felt for him. Surely no one had
been thoughtless enough to say such a thing to him. 'I
am very sorry,' she said. 'I wouldn't be working in an
eye hospital if I didn't know the value of one's sight.'

Lee shrugged, then with his hands dug deep into his
trouser pockets he slumped on to the bed.

'I wouldn't care if I'd been one of 'em,' he said

viciously, then beating one fist into the palm of his other hand he went on: 'but I wasn't, blondie, I wasn't.'

His voice croaked and Valda went at once to his side. She noticed that he'd changed his trousers. Had someone been to see him, his mother perhaps?

'It isn't any of my business what happened, Lee, but if you want to talk . . .'

'Talk!' he yelled bitterly. 'What the hell is there to talk about?'

'I understand how you feel,' she consoled.

'No, you don't. Nobody understands—only me! I was there, caught up in a brawl that had nothing to do with me. I came up to the lights at Fallow Cross and these two guys fighting fell out into the road in front of me, then all hell exploded. Bottles and knives—they tore me off my motorbike, smashed it to ruin and that's all I remember.'

'You didn't know any of them?'

Lee shook his head. 'No, this isn't my patch and anyway I don't belong to any gang, I told you, I'm a loner. I saw enough fighting in my own home not to want to get involved myself.'

There was an awkward pause before Valda asked: 'Have you had visitors, Lee? Your mother perhaps?'

'No—why?'

'You've changed your trousers,' Valda observed.

Lee suddenly laughed aloud.

'If the Sister of this ward hadn't been so bitchy this morning she'd have taken the trouble to find out why I was in the bathroom with my jeans unzipped.'

'Actually I thought it was rather obvious,' Valda joked.

He turned to look at her directly. 'It might have been if you'd been with me. Oh, the nurses are all right, fun and all that, but I don't make instant relationships of that sort, and all we were doing was trying to make my zip work. It was kind of you to get them cleaned but they loused up the zip.'

Valda laughed too. 'Oh dear, and you had to go into Mr Carr like that.'

'Yes, but he was very understanding and he went off somewhere and borrowed these pants for me.'

Valda was suddenly serious. 'Lee, your mother, we should notify her.'

'The police are doing that. Oh, blondie, I'm not a down-and-out. I want to work and live a decent life.'

Valda went to sit down on the chair by the window. He was ready to talk and she was a patient, willing listener.

It was some time later when the supper trolley came round that Valda felt able to leave Lee. She still had to finish the day report and Nurse Rippon had found her to say that Caroline and her mother had just arrived. After a few words with Mrs Royston who was to stay in with five-year-old Caroline Valda completed the paperwork, and Pam Gardner and the second-year pupil nurse arrived to take over.

Valda was thankful to get off duty and went to the canteen where she sat down to a large helping of spaghetti bolognese followed by a somewhat stodgy but delicious ginger pudding with a syrupy sauce. She was washing it all down with her second cup of coffee when a shadow fell across the table. To her astonishment it was Sebastian Carr. There was only the flicker of a smile on his face as his gaze roved over the empty plates.

'How do you do it?' he mocked, 'eat like a schoolgirl and keep that trim figure?'

To anyone else she'd have probably quipped that it wasn't as trim as she would like, but she was at a loss for words at his unexpected intrusion.

'Finished?' he asked smugly at her lack of response.

'Almost,' she said, flashing her blue eyes speculatively.

'Drink up then, I want you.'

'What for?' she asked with a puzzled frown.

Sebastian sighed. 'Just hurry up,' he said, implying

that she was being tiresome.

She calmly—as calmly as her fluttering heartbeats would allow—drank the remains of her coffee, then picked up her leather bag, slung it over one shoulder and stood up.

He led the way in his distinctive brisk manner, his lithe figure moving sensuously beneath the charcoal grey suit he was wearing, through the corridor to an adjoining one which led into the now silent outpatients department.

The whole of the front of the old hospital building had been re-modernised and divided up into the various rooms required for ear, nose, throat and eye casualty. Behind that area lay the vast outpatients clinics, and along the back overlooking the garden were the kitchens, domestic quarters and dining-room from which they had just come.

Faint distant sounds came from the casualty section but Sebastian went to his outpatient consulting room and unlocked the door. He indicated that Valda should precede him and now that her mind had cleared she recalled that he had promised to continue their conversation of earlier in the day.

She experienced a shudder of awe. A shouting match with him was surely going to start her head thumping again. He'd chosen the quiet of this deserted department so that they wouldn't be overheard, she supposed.

Valda was aware that he had simply given the door a push so that it was still ajar as he went straight to his desk.

'You can sit if you like,' he suggested vaguely, but Valda decided to remain standing as he did. A large brown paper parcel lay opened on the desk and now he drew from it reams of paper.

'Merle's been over this evening, she's done a grand job with the sponsorship forms, and publicity posters. Have you had any thoughts about how you'll make sure every member of the staff gets one?'

She had been staring at the top of his head, secretly admiring the blend of highlights which shaded his light brown hair.

Now his eyes surveyed her in close scrutiny, and the faint flush that came and went swiftly to her cheeks he took as a sign of rebellion. He lay both hands flat on the crackling brown paper and his face levelled with hers threateningly.

'Valda,' he said sternly, 'I am simply *not* going to tolerate your stubbornness. The more you fight me the more work I shall give you to do. Everyone else has bent over backwards to co-operate. Everyone that is, except you. I don't understand. Do you find me that insufferable to work with?'

CHAPTER SEVEN

VALDA had to lower her gaze to the desk. She couldn't bear it. His closeness had brought about an honesty that was too revealing. How could she say: 'I love you and I'll do anything you want me to?' Her throat constricted, her voice muscles seemed to have tightened into a knot. She really was reacting like a moonstruck teenager, she reproached herself.

Sebastian ran an impatient hand through his wavy hair in growing anger.

'Damn it, Valda—what have I done?' He banged his hand down on the reams of coloured paper. 'Has the cat got your tongue?' he roared.

Valda pressed her cold fingertips to her temple.

'Please don't shout, Mr Carr,' he said. 'I've had a dreadful headache all day. I can't think straight tonight.'

He sat down and placed elegant hands over his face briefly.

'I'm sorry,' he murmured softly. 'You should have said you weren't well.'

'I'm perfectly all right,' she argued quickly if illogically. 'I . . . I just have a tendency to headaches.'

She dared to let her eyes meet his. His gaze didn't falter and as he let his hands fall to the parcel again where he casually linked his fingers together she saw the beginnings of a bewitching smile.

'I thought that was an excuse peculiar to married women,' he said, then with a shake of his head in self-reproach he added: 'Forgive me, I didn't mean to be facetious.'

There was a dreadfully long silence before he asked: 'Have you taken anything to relieve the pain?'

Valda's heart leapt in agony. What, among all the hundreds of pain-killing drugs, was there to cure heartache?

'I had some aspirins earlier and a good sleep this afternoon.' She shrugged. 'It's nothing—really.'

'I disagree. Perhaps you need your eyes tested. You do have a considerable amount of paperwork to do now that you're a Sister.'

Valda sighed. 'I don't mind that, at least I'm sitting down. It's been more difficult lately now that we've gone to a thirty-seven and a half hour week. It's a time consuming job working out off duties which have to be done so far in advance.'

A lame excuse she thought, but the only one she could come up with on the spur of the moment.

'But you do get more off duty now so I don't think I'm asking too much of you to enlist your help?' he pleaded.

'I said I'd help,' she said.

'But you sound so unwilling, Valda.' She didn't answer. Of course she had been unwilling. From that first meeting hadn't she been trying to fight off the truth which now refused to be ignored?

Sebastian smiled gently. Oh, God, how it tormented her!

'Maybe I really don't understand you as well as I thought I did.' He surveyed the bulky paper package again and folded the wrapping over the clean sheets. 'They're here—whenever you can manage to pick them up.'

'I'll take them into the dining-room in the morning,' she assured him, 'and I'll put up a notice asking everyone to make sure they get one.' Her conscience pricked. Turncoat, she thought maliciously. She was a hypocrite. No, that was what she *had* been, now she was behaving more honestly.

Another long interlude passed, not stretching between them in division but rather drawing them together on a more compatible level. Sebastian arched his smooth black eyebrows and his even white teeth gleamed between his sensuous lips.

'Are you in a hurry?'

Valda hesitated. She was anxious to have an early night, but suddenly it was important to her to stay with Sebastian.

'Not specially,' she replied cautiously. 'I was going to ring my father to find out how Miss Kepple is, and if he's missing his little companion.'

'There'll be time for that,' Sebastian said, rising to his feet. 'Howard keeps late hours. A short drive might blow that headache away. I'd like to show you something.' He came round to Valda's side of the desk, and with an arm round her shoulder guided her firmly to the door.

It was still light as they walked to the huge car-park which spanned the distance between the old and new hospitals. He opened the passenger door of his car, settling her in comfortably before sitting beside her, and they travelled in almost total silence going in the direction which usually took her home to Deasley. Surely he wasn't intending to visit Maple Cottage this late, but at the road junction where the sign publicised Miranda's kennels and cattery he took the road towards it. A crazy fear flooded through Valda. Did he live with Miranda for much of the time? Where they secretly married? What could be the purpose of taking Valda there at this time of night?

But before they came to the lane which led to Miranda's bungalow Sebastian took a right-hand turn which was nothing more than a bumpy gravel track. In the gathering dusk it resembled a builders yard, Valda thought, and as Sebastian pulled on to some grass she could see there was in fact a half-built house on the site.

As he opened her door he flicked her cap.

'Take that off,' he commanded, 'you're off duty now.'

She did as he requested, tossing it on to the back seat, and he helped her out of the car. It was magic just to feel his hand at her elbow as he led her towards the building.

'Thank goodness we've had a spell of good weather so the ground is dry, but it's uneven so take care. And at last the builders have been able to get cracking. Not that there's a great deal to see as yet, and in this half-light—still—it's mine. What do you think?' he asked, nurturing a touch of pride.

Valda felt her heart sinking fast. People go in for property when they're thinking of marriage, and she was reminded that this land backed on to Miranda's. It was becoming clinically obvious.

'I'm sure it'll be very nice,' she replied in a soft voice.

Sebastian laughed. 'It had better be, it's costing me the earth. I realise that you can't get much of an idea from only this much, but if they adhere to the plans it should be a semi-bungalow of character. Perhaps chalet-style would be a more apt description. The land here is slightly higher so we're to have a cellar or basement, the lounge will have sliding doors to a patio. Um—dining-room, utility room and kitchen,' he explained, waving his arm in various directions. 'Bathroom, showers in the two main bedrooms, and two good sized rooms upstairs with a bathroom, then at the side over the garage I shall have a consulting room, small waiting hall and the usual offices.'

Valda was grateful that it was getting dark so that he couldn't see her stony expression. Evidently he was thinking of marriage in the not too distant future, and a family, judging by the size of the place, and in his spare time, like most consultants he would see patients privately.

'Your wife will be a very lucky lady then,' Valda ventured to say.

Sebastian sighed and issued a vague kind of 'Yes.'

He had a way of standing, feet slightly apart, both

hands under his jacket tucked in the back waistband of his trousers. In the peace of the countryside she could hear the chink of his watch chain as he swayed slightly from side to side surveying his future home.

Valda looked across at him and the stirrings of her heart warned her of dangerous desires. She longed to place her fingers over his heart to feel the rhythmic beat which she felt sure she could persuade into uncontrollable pounding. She had an irresistible desire to tousle his hair and to tease his lips with hers. But those pleasures must be Miranda's. He half-turned and met her stare, then in a soft voice he asked: 'You think it would be wasted on a lonely bachelor then, Valda?'

Her heart missed not one beat but two or three. Could she be wrong about him and Miranda, or was this to be a place he could bring a variety of women? He had a certain reputation, she remembered.

'Not if it's what you want,' she said.

'I want the lady of my choice to love it as much as I do—and I'm pretty sure she will.'

Valda turned away, unable to cope with his self-satisfaction. She knew he was studying her solemn face and they remained apart from one another for several minutes. Then in a low voice he asked: 'Headache gone?'

She nodded. She dare not speak as she knew her voice was bound to make public her heartache.

He took a side-step nearer to her. 'Then I won't be committing any great crime if I—kiss you?' he asked hesitantly. It was a question of uncertainty; what else might he have wanted to do? she wondered.

Everything about her began to whirl and then his strong arms were supporting her. He held her as if he was afraid she might break at his touch, but when their lips met it was as if a flare went up. There was only one thing to do with her hands and arms and that was to encircle his body and draw him closer, and as his lips moved over hers she felt his hard muscular desire urging her body to respond. But she fought against his persua-

sion. He was Miranda's, and she belonged to Adrian.
When he paused Sebastian smiled down at her.
'Moonlight was made for kissing,' he whispered, and
then as if he could no longer contain himself he kissed
her more passionately, his powerful hands pressing her
body close to his until a shudder forced him to release
her. He took her by the hand and led her back to the
car.

'You must come with me again and watch how the
work progresses,' he said, and as she fiddled with the
seat belt, her eyes smarting from unshed tears, he got
into the driver's seat and placing a warm, comforting
hand over her knee added: 'It must be this country air.
Deasley has a lot to answer for.'

Valda didn't know how to reply, if indeed she was
expected to, but later when she felt better able to trust
herself to speak she said: 'At least you'll be near to
your sister if she needs your help.'

Sebastian laughed, and said with a hint of sarcasm,
'A little too close I expect you mean, but Jessica's not
so bad. She dislikes me having my Addlefield flat, but I
simply couldn't put up with her all the time. I've always
had my freedom and I guard it jealously. She's only
thirty-two and it's right that she should bring the boys
up her way, but she may well marry again.'

'She has sons?' Valda asked.

'The two boys you saw at the strawberry field. They're
her stepsons. Frank was a widower, you see, but he's
left Jess with few problems, their education is all set up.
Frank saw to that. They go to boarding school so
they'll gradually drift away to a life of their own, but
at present they're good boys and are company for
Jessica. At least they'll keep her off my back for a bit.'

Valda was forced to smile. He thought he was being
a caring brother when really Jessica mothered him. She
had warned Valda of his reputation for breaking hearts.
Did she know about Miranda and the new house? It
wasn't a question she could ask Sebastian. *She* knew,

and pretty downcast the knowledge made her. Yet she wondered why he was so drawn to holding her and kissing her when only a few yards away he could have found Miranda. He was a man full of mystery and that, she supposed, was his attraction.

When they drew up outside Conifer Lodge he unstrapped himself. 'I'd better see you safely in,' he said with a laugh.

'There's really no need,' Valda protested, but she was glad when he put his arm around her and walked her up the drive.

'Goodnight, sweet Nordic beauty,' he whispered when they reached the door, 'and I hope that from now on we shan't be fighting each other. I want the laser machine paid for inside six months so we're going to pull all the stops out. Oh, I almost forgot—I owe you an apology.'

Valda turned to him with a perplexed expression.

'You were right about Lee—there's a lot of good in him,' Sebastian said. 'He's had a rough deal so he needs all the help we can give him—but don't let him get too fond of you.'

'Not much chance of that,' Valda said with amusement.

He kissed her suddenly. 'There's every chance of that, you have no idea what you do to us men. Busy day tomorrow—so until then, sweet dreams,' and he strode back to his car.

Valda realised when she got up to her room that she felt quite light-headed. He had magicked away her headache and made her feel just a little bit special. Why should he have chosen her to show off the house to? Miranda might not like it. Valda knew she wouldn't if she were in Miranda's shoes. If only she were! She knew now though that it was useless her loving Sebastian the way she did, but how did she stop? She stood at the window trying to think of other things like how long would the lovely weather last, but her thoughts simply went full circle on a merry-go-round and she was back to her desperate plight. Rain or shine she couldn't help but brood over her feelings for the consultant. She ought to do what her father had suggested and move away. Go to a different hospital where she could start afresh. Her father had suggested it though because he was trying to break up her romance with Adrian. Was he using Sebastian to do it for him? No, that was unthinkable. Her father would never stoop to such methods. All the same someone or something had come between her and Adrian. It was Merle, Valda decided, trying to absolve herself from blame. Merle had been into the hospital today—had Adrian accompanied her? Valda was furious with herself for her jealousy, but Adrian was hers. And yet she loved Sebastian, and loving him could only mean torment and unrequited love. She suddenly felt lonely for Adrian. They enjoyed each other's company, or had done until Merle had become noticeable. Why should she just let him go? Wasn't it up to her to hang on to Adrian like grim death? If she didn't want to lose him she must see that she didn't!

Valda didn't phone her father; instead she went to bed and allowed nostalgia to give her the sweet dreams Sebastian had wished for her. Tomorrow she would contact Adrian.

A theatre day meant little time for dwelling on one's love life and as Valda stood at her desk next morning soon after seven-thirty, rolling up her sleeves to put on her arm bands, she was confronted by an angry Pam Gardner.

'I know it was one of those 'let's jigger eye-wards' days yesterday, Val, but surely someone could have made sure that Mrs Royston got the telephone trolley she asked for?'

Valda looked puzzled. 'She didn't ask me for one.

Let's see, I think I assigned Nurse Rippon to see them settled in.'

'When I eventually got round to them at about ten o'clock the poor woman was still waiting to phone her husband.'

'Perhaps it's just as well for Nurse Rippon that this is another day—I'd had enough of her tomfoolery yesterday so I might have been tempted to be a bitch and report her to the SNO, but she will have to be severely reprimanded. I'll send her to apologise to Mrs Royston and I'll have a word myself. Was it too late to ring Mr Royston?'

'No—she got through all right, but Caroline should have been asleep by then. Mrs Royston is, not unnaturally, worried on Caroline's account, and apparently getting here turned out to be something of an event. Her car broke down so she had to call out the breakdown services and there she was on a country road waiting for hours.'

'She was late getting in, that's why I didn't really have time to spare her when she did arrive. Caroline is all prepared, I take it?'

'Yes, nil by mouth after midnight and she's in her angel gown, and the bed made up. I gave her pre-med at seven. Lee also is ready—you know, he's not so bad, in fact I rather like him. He's sensible really.'

'His attitude in the beginning was all for bravado I expect,' Valda said. 'He's a victim of circumstance I believe.'

'He's been quite restless through the night so I've tried to calm him and he seems to be accepting the fact that it's better to lose an eye now than possibly the sight in the other eye later. It's tragic though, he's so young.'

'If I get time I'll ring Dad today. He came yesterday to fetch Miss Kepple and he knew Lee, but I was so tied up I didn't have time to ask how.'

'Playing Cupid, are we?' Pam asked with a smirk.

Valda laughed. 'Miss Kepple and Dad? Not me—Carlos might, perhaps. Miss Kepple's rather sweet, but I don't think Dad wants a woman round him all the time. He's even trying to get rid of me.'

'But you don't see him all that often, do you?'

'Only every other weekend when I'm off, but I get the impression that he doesn't like Adrian. Last time I went home he suggested I mustn't stop in this area for his benefit. If I wanted to go off to pastures new he wouldn't mind.'

'Perhaps he meant if you and Adrian were to get married.'

Valda gave Pam a sidelong glance. 'No, somehow I don't think he did mean that. Oh, he'd be happy for me if Adrian and I did decide to make it together, but I know my Dad and it's not what he says, it's the unspoken words that count.'

'But it's your life, Valda.'

'Exactly—and at the moment my life has been taken over by this laser appeal. Here's your form, by the way. I took them to the dining-room at breakfast time and I'm going to visit all the wards today and leave some so that everyone gets one. There's also a large notice on display in the dining-room saying that jogging will be a group effort. Every morning at six-thirty for the day staff, and every evening at seven-thirty for you lot.'

Pam made a face. 'Well,' she said, 'I know I could do with losing a few pounds, but jogging—uh!'

'I expected to get a lot of moans when I distributed the sponsorship forms, but surprisingly nearly everyone was enthusiastic.'

'Who wouldn't be with the adorable Mr Carr organising things, especially as I'm told he takes part and is a really good sport. Duncan told me he's organising a football match later on for the appeal and will be playing on the field.'

Valda shrugged. 'He's formed a committee but he doesn't need one as he does all the organising himself.

Still, it saves anyone else the bother.' She sat down at the desk as the day nurses began to gather round to listen to the report, and when she had finished she said: 'I'm off for the afternoon so Sister O'Brien will be here I expect to help Staff Nurse Adey.' As the girls began to drift away to start the day's work Valda called Nurse Rippon back. 'Will you wait here a moment, I want a word with you.'

The night staff left and Valda asked the junior nurse why she hadn't finished her work before she went off duty the previous day. The girl looked completely nonplussed until Valda reminded her of Mrs Royston's request for a telephone trolley, then she clapped a hand to her mouth.

'It may have seemed inconsequential to you, Nurse, but Mrs Royston had problems getting here so naturally she wanted to contact her husband,' Valda said.

'She could have gone to the day room herself and looked for the telephone,' Nurse Rippon said defiantly.

'That's not the point,' Valda argued crossly. 'If you can't be bothered to remember such a simple request how are you going to be responsible in more important issues?'

Nurse Rippon looked at the floor, a guilty flush spreading into her cheeks, and at that moment a decisive tread could be heard as Sebastian Carr walked into the office just as Valda continued: 'You must go at once to Mrs Royston and apologise, and while we're on the subject of discipline, Nurse, there seems to be a tendency with you and Nurse Dickson to think nursing is some sort of game. It's a profession with a reputation of the highest degree and I expect to see you both working with more diligence and sense of responsibility in future.'

In the middle of this tirade Valda glanced at the doorway where Sebastian had come to a halt. He raised his eyebrows and made a grimace at Valda's sharp tone, but his eyes were alight with laughter. Valda ignored him and turned to Nurse Rippon again.

'I shall be watching you both closely from now on, and I hope you'll remember that it's necessary for me to give a detailed report of your progress at the end of the month. It's just as well for you that I haven't got to do it today. I'll see Nurse Dickson myself shortly. Now go to room three and when you've apologised to Mrs Royston you can assist Staff Nurse Adey with the theatre list.'

The girl went away in silence, though it was evident that she was bursting to retaliate.

Sebastian came up to the desk. 'Not another headache today?' he teased.

Valda smiled. 'No—or I couldn't have said all that. I try to sort out such problems when I'm feeling rational. They think because I'm young they can get away with murder.'

'I'm glad to see that you take your responsibilities with such inexorable dedication. How did the forms go down?'

'On the whole quite well—one or two moans, but most of those I've seen so far seem willing to take part. I finish at midday today so I'll go over to the new hospital after lunch and leave some on every ward.'

'Good girl. I'll be ready to start in about fifteen minutes.'

She looked up at him and savoured the affectionate smile he gave her. That and the laughter in his eyes would carry her through the next twenty-four hours. She couldn't comprehend how he could look at her like that, kiss her with such force, and yet be preparing to marry Miranda. She sighed disconsolately. It wasn't that hard to fathom out, he simply needed her help. All the same he had no reason for taking her out to see his new house last evening. But then again, she reasoned, he probably had been going himself anyway, and having shouted at her when she was in a frail condition he felt he was appeasing his ill-temper, and at the same time, more importantly, winning her round for his cause.

He'd certainly done that, she ruminated, casting a disconcerting eye over the pile of sponsorship forms on the corner of her desk. But even the great Mr Carr had to put aside the laser appeal for the moment. The theatre bell ringing at intervals throughout the morning kept the eye-wards busy, and Valda had cause to be grateful that Mrs Royston was on hand to pacify Caroline and tend to her needs during the post-operative period.

It was after lunch and almost two o'clock when Valda turned her direction away from the old hospital building, and coming out of the dining-room she walked through the covered way which linked the old hospital to the new. As she visited each ward and department she felt a little envious of the ultra-modern newness of everywhere. Some of the staff she had trained with, many of the older ward sisters and supervisors she had worked under and been disciplined by in the early days, but everyone greeted her pleasantly and she felt a sense of well-being at having reached the point in her career where she could feel confident and free to converse with the older staff on their own level.

By the time she reached the downstairs casualty and outpatients departments she felt as if she had been recruited to take an active part in all the fund-raising. Morale was high and enthusiasm overwhelming; she couldn't persuade others to participate if she wasn't prepared to set an example just as Sebastian Carr had said. And why should everyone else have all the fun? No one could possibly know how she craved to be near the compelling consultant, and if that was the only reason that they were all anxious to share in his crusade, it was a good enough reason for her too.

She was crossing the car-park and making for Conifer Lodge when she recognised Adrian's car sliding into a space on the far side reserved for visitors to the Pathological Laboratory. By the way he waved and leaned on the top of his car she guessed that he had seen her before she had noticed him. At the sight of the sunlight dancing on his sleek black hair, and his tall, lean frame and handsome features Valda's heart danced with joy, and she broke into a run.

Adrian laughed. 'Careful, darling, don't overdo it,' he said as he walked to meet her.'

'Can I interest you in a sponsorship form?' she asked, laughing up at him.

'Already got mine. Merle's into this thing with great gusto so she's badgering us all to do the sponsored swim.'

Valda tried not to let her jealousy show as she maintained her cheerfulness. 'What are you doing here?' she asked.

'One of my patients has suspected pernicious anaemia so I've brought the blood sample in myself to get a quick result.'

'I'm off for the rest of today, thank goodness,' she said.

'So I'd have gone up to eye wards on a fool's errand? Why didn't you ring?'

'I didn't have time this morning, but I was going to in a few minutes from Conifer Lodge. I suppose you've got a surgery this evening?'

'I have, but if you're free I'll make an early start and I'll talk all my patients out of being poorly and insist that they sponsor me in the swim instead. That way they'll be only to anxious to get out of my clutches.'

They laughed together. It was like it had been before —they *were* compatible, eager to please one another, enjoying life in a light-hearted way, fully understanding each other. Before what? a little voice prompted. Before Sebastian Carr had come on the scene, and Merle Decarta, but the sun was shining extraordinarily brightly today and she felt that everything was right.

'I ought to go home,' she said. 'I was going to phone Dad but if I'm going to join the joggers I shall need my track suit, that's if I can still get into it!'

Adrian's black eyes never left her smiling face. He looked as if he wanted to kiss her, but whereas once Valda would have taken the initiative she restrained herself, and he was guarding his reputation.

'You might need to let something out somewhere,' Adrian said jovially. 'Myself, I'd rather see you in a swimsuit.'

Valda tapped his lips. 'A taboo subject,' she said.

'Lets go for a meal, darling?' Adrian said, suddenly more serious. 'Somewhere quiet and secluded where we can be alone, we get so little time to talk without being interrupted.'

She knew what he meant. So far in their relationship they met at Maple Cottage or at the Jester inn, but always there was someone around. On the few rare occasions that she went to his flat there seemed to be a prevailing undercurrent of unease. She found it easy to be provocative with Adrian anywhere but at his flat, and now she felt she didn't ever want to go there again because it might be Merle who would interrupt them.

'All right,' she agreed instantly. 'I'll have a cup of tea with Dad and come back to Addlefield about seven-thirty. Where shall we meet?'

'Come to the Health Centre about seven. Let's make the most of the evening—if you don't mind taking me as I am, I may not get the opportunity to go home to change.'

Valda had gone home only to find her father out. She was almost glad, and after searching out her track suit, running shoes, shorts and tee-shirt she had written him a note and then departed.

On reaching Conifer Lodge she tried on her track suit which apart from being a little too well fitting round the top half of her was still wearable, so she went for half an hour's practice run before showering and making herself attractive for Adrian. This time, she told herself severely, I'm dressing up for Adrian, not Sebastian Carr.

Almost any colour suited her blonde hair which she brushed vigorously so that it sprang up in big curls which dangled on her shoulders. She smiled to herself at Adrian suggesting he might look less than his best, for he always looked immaculate in lounge suits which made him appear distinguished.

She decided to wear a dainty voile dress, one of the few garments she had not made herself, but had purchased in a sale at an exclusive gown shop in the old part of Addlefield long before the one-way system had divided the small town. She had saved it to wear on a special occasion. She didn't know why today was the day, but she felt the time was right. The colours were predominantly silver-grey and jade green in a floral design, the style classically simple, a plunging neckline, tight fitting bodice, billowing sleeves, with a concertina pleated skirt. A wide grey shiny belt showed off her slim waist and at last she could wear some rather frivolous high-heeled grey patent leather shoes she had bought at the same time. Surveying herself in the mirror she decided that whatever she'd worn, even in her Sister's uniform, she felt good tonight. But she refused to admit that the new compatible relationship with the crusading consultant had anything at all to do with it.

Now, having parked her car behind the Health Centre, she was sitting beside Adrian. It had been an easy evening surgery he explained as they drove along, and he'd finished in good time. He'd also had time to return to his flat at five o'clock, shower and change into a lightweight natural coloured suit with a dark brown shirt and matching patterned tie which gave him a continental look.

Valda knew from local gossip that he cut quite a dash with patients at the Centre, and was much sought after not only because of his general appeal but because he had a gentle, understanding manner.

'Where are we going?' Valda asked excitedly as he turned on to the motorway. She expected him to have

booked a table at one of the local restaurants, or even
at the Jester inn, but he was speeding away from
Addlefield, and as they chatted she guessed that he was
making for somewhere quiet in the country. Eventually
they reached some old thatched properties that had
been made into an exclusive restaurant near the river.

Conversation flowed as easily as the shimmering water
with seemingly no inhibitions. They were alone together,
away from all other distractions, and the delicious
steaks were enjoyed, as was the vintage wine Adrian
insisted upon, while soft romantic melodies hung
pleasurably in the air. After selecting light whipped
cream delicacies from the dessert trolley they waited for
coffee and liqueurs, and with shining eyes faced each
other over the flickering candle. Adrian stretched out
his hands and caught Valda's, holding them tenderly.

There was something different about him tonight, she
thought, and the fond feeling she had always felt for
him seemed to be strengthening.

'I do love you,' he mouthed. The almost inaudible
sound could scarcely be called a whisper, and Valda
was so overcome with emotion that she felt a girlish
blush crimson her cheeks. She didn't doubt for one
moment that he was genuine, and then he caressed her
hands with his thumb and leaned forward more closely,
beginning: 'I said—'

'I know what you said,' she breathed. 'You've never
said it before.'

The waiter brought coffee and liqueurs, and the
moment of reckoning passed. She tried to convince
herself that she loved him, but she was unable to tell a
lie. She was impressed with his hypnotic charm and she
knew she was eager to fall under his spell, but now
there was Sebastian.

Adrian stirred his coffee thoughtfully. 'Have you
thought any more about joining the club?' he asked.

Valda knew she must steer the conversation back to
one of light-hearted banter. She giggled. 'I could ask,

which one?'

Adrian laughed briefly, then his expression became sober as he leaned back in his chair.

'I mean it, darling. We should see one another more often, and it would help you to get in shape for all those sporting activities your Mr Carr is devising.'

She silently challenged the 'your Mr Carr'. He could never be hers. For one thing she doubted that he would want her, and he was Miranda's.

'Give me time, darling,' she begged. 'I know you want me to swim and I honestly wish I could, but I lack the courage. Perhaps I'd feel safer in the sea. It's a pity we don't live nearer the coast.'

'It's not impossible to visit a seaside resort,' he suggested casually. 'This weather is supposed to last until the end of the month so we ought to make the most of it. How about a weekend away?'

It sounded like heaven and she darted him a quizzical look. 'You mean—?' she began warily.

He leaned forward, gazing directly into her blue eyes. She felt as if he were searching for some profound truth.

'I mean a weekend in a hotel—and don't be naïve enough to ask me to book single rooms, they're like gold dust and cost too much. What might or might not take place is up to us. You're off this weekend, so how about it?'

CHAPTER EIGHT

ADRIAN'S suggestion was so unexpected that Valda was stunned to silence, and then in a desperate bid to keep the compatible conversation going she asked: 'Are you off too then?'

A pretty waitress interrupted at that moment with a basket of chocolates and mints to which they were invited to help themselves.

Adrian popped a mint into his mouth and fed Valda across the table with a chocolate. 'Bribery,' he said lightly. 'If you promise me you'll say 'yes' you can have my chocolate.'

Valda was sitting with her mouth open and the chocolate was held just out of her grasp until they were both laughing helplessly.

'Of course I'm off too, silly,' Adrian said, finally letting her take the chocolate between her teeth.

'It sounds a wonderful idea, but it's a bit short notice,' she said.

He waved a warning finger at her. 'Just get your bikini ready,' he said, 'leave the rest to me. After next weekend, God willing, weather permitting,' he paused, placing his hands together and raising his dark eyes heavenwards, 'you'll be as keen to swim as the rest of us.'

'Don't expect too much of me, darling, please.' There was a note of reticence in Valda's voice. She knew that Adrian understood that she wasn't speaking about swimming. A week or a so ago she had thought they were drifting apart, but now Adrian was making every effort to persuade her that there was some commitment to a deeper relationship. She tried to convince herself

that it was what she wanted, had wanted ever since she
and Adrian had met. Sebastian Carr was like a devil
who had come to tempt her and for a while it seemed
that she had given in, but now she had things in their
right perspective. The consultant was a clever, scheming
philanderer who could charm his way into anyone's
heart. She admitted having been flattered by his attention, which she realised was merely a way of ensuring
her co-operation. How much more dependable Adrian
was. She knew exactly where she stood with him, and
somehow the thought of a secure and steady future
seemed infinitely more appealing than wondering what
state of mind Sebastian Carr would be in next time they
met.

The evening ended on a note of happiness and promise
as Adrian held her close and whispered again that he
loved her. Finally she got out of Adrian's silver-grey
Cortina and unlocked the door of her small Honda.

'I hate you having to drive yourself home after an
evening out, darling,' Adrian said. 'Take care. I'll give
you a ring as soon as I've got a confirmed booking
somewhere.'

He bent to kiss her again, and Valda hummed a love
song as she drove back to the hospital and Conifer
Lodge.

She was glad she was on late shift the following day
so that she was able to sleep for an extra hour, but then
the sun was shining again and she felt uplifted at the
anticipation of a weekend away with Adrian, though
she experienced some slight reserve at how her father
would react.

She did her few bits of washing, looked out things
suitable for taking to the coast even though it was a
week away, and as she prepared for going on duty at
midday she listened to the radio which helped to keep
her mind occupied.

Valda took a detailed report from Staff Nurse Adey
as soon as she reached the ward, though this was

interrupted a few times by the clanging of a bell which turned out to be young Caroline playing with the bell over her bed.

'Little monkey,' Staff Nurse Adey grumbled after the third interruption. 'Her mother's gone out for a breath of fresh air and Caroline is able to understand enough to know that pressing a button summons the entire nursing staff.'

They went carefully through the list of patients until they reached Lee Abbott's name.

'How is he?' Valda asked with concern.

'Drops and ointment as prescribed, we've kept the socket clean. He's all right, but doesn't seem inclined to mix much now.'

'Understandable in a way, although all our patients are Nelsons with a bandage or shield over one eye, so at least he's no different from the rest. No word from his mother, I suppose?'

'I haven't heard anything. The social worker has been to see him and I think they've arranged for him to go to a hostel when he's discharged.'

'Rotten for him, isn't it?' Valda said. 'You're too old at nineteen to be taken into care, yet how can a lad like Lee cope on his own, especially with no job?'

'He'll need special care when he gets out of here in a few days' time. He'll feel so isolated, but there's not much we can do. Did your dad know anything about his background?' Staff Nurse Adey asked.

'I didn't see my father,' Valda explained, and then the bell pealed through the corridors again.

The staff nurse groaned, but Valda intervened. 'I'll go. She can come round the ward with me. I suppose her mother will be back soon.'

Five-year-old Caroline was kneeling up playing with the bell which was on a long cord but which the nursing staff had tied up. This hadn't deterred Caroline though.

'It's stuck,' she announced proudly.

Valda took a look, but no amount of pressing, poking

or shaking would release it.

Nurses came from everywhere, but no one could solve the problem.

'Better fetch a porter or electrician, or someone from maintenance,' Valda suggested, and as she hurried down the corridor from room three she bumped into Lee Abbott who was peering out of the door of his room.

'What's all the bloody racket?' he asked gruffly.

'Hallo, Lee—oh, I wonder if you can help?' she urged. 'Caroline's pressed her bell and we can't stop it.'

She led the way back again and within seconds Lee had taken the thing to pieces and stopped the ringing.

'Oh, thanks,' Valda said gratefully. 'What a relief.'

'You've got a patch like me,' Caroline said to Lee. 'My teddy's had an operation too and he's got a patch as well.'

Lee paused. Valda could almost hear her own heart beating loudly as she waited for some sort of oath from Lee, but he was slowly beginning to smile and then he picked up Caroline's teddy bear.

Valda slipped away with Caroline's happy chatter in her ears. At least Lee couldn't be rude to a child, neither did he have to make polite conversation.

Valda visited all her patients in the main ward in turn then, taking care to observe and listen carefully to their version of their condition. She had reached Mr Stanford's bedside and was making the elderly gentleman comfortable when she heard footsteps coming along the corridor.

It was several minutes before anyone came to look for Valda and then to a peal of babyish laughter a teddy bear's head came into view in the doorway, and a funny voice called: 'Hallo, Sister. Caroline's got her patch off, can I have mine off too?' The voice was an excellent mimicry of Punch and Judy and even dear old Mr Stanford laughed.

Valda went to the doorway. 'You'll have to ask Mr Carr, teddy,' she said.

'I want Sister to take my bandage off,' came the plaintive cry.

The teddy bear bobbed forward to hit Valda on the nose. She laughed as she followed Sebastian and Caroline across the corridor to room three.

Mrs Royston came puffing in as the eye patches were dispensed with. 'Sorry I've been such ages,' she apologised breathlessly. 'I hope Caroline hasn't given you any trouble?'

'No,' Valda said with tongue in cheek, 'she's been fine.'

Sebastian played a game with Caroline, a game which incorporated looking at her eye, then he said, 'I expect you'd like to go home now, wouldn't you, Caroline?'

'I don't mind it here,' she said, 'as long as Mummy can stay too.'

'Well, I think teddy is quite well now, and he assures me that he wants to go home.' Sebastian glanced across at Mrs Royston. 'Tomorrow morning you can leave, Mrs Royston. Sister here will see that you get an appointment for outpatients clinic in a couple of weeks, so I'll see Caroline then.'

As they left the small room Valda said: 'Are you doing a round now?'

'Yes, Sister, if you'll accompany me.' He smiled his most devastatingly disarming smile.

'I'll go and get the notes trolley,' she said. 'Consultants usually do their round in the morning.'

Sebastian raised his eyebrows. 'Well, today *I'm* doing it in the afternoon,' he informed her slowly. 'It doesn't always do to be anticipated.'

From his look Valda could have surmised that he was suggesting he had left it purposely to do when she was on duty, but she dispelled this idea as preposterous. She was flattering herself again! In a leisurely fashion the consultant visited every patient and when they eventually returned to the office he finished writing on the last patient's notes at Valda's desk. Then he sat back and toyed with his pen.

'You appear to be in top form again, Sister?' he observed.

'After a half-day off duty I should be,' she quipped with a radiant smile.

'But not enough to join the jogging team this morning?'

'I went for a short run yesterday at tea-time, but I had a lie-in this morning.'

'Out on the town last evening, I suppose.' It wasn't a question, just the great man voicing his thoughts as an aside.

'Adrian and I did go out for a meal.' Valda felt that it was the right time to remind him that she had a boy-friend, and she was determined that her relationship with the consultant would mean that she could converse in a friendly manner.

With his usual direct stare he managed to make Valda feel as if she had no right to have gone out with Adrian.

'We shall have to have a celebration meal when we've bought the laser machine. Did Adrian tell you that the Health Centre has already collected over two hundred pounds? Merle tells me that various patients are producing things to raffle.'

'No,' she admitted. 'Adrian didn't mention it.'

'Other fish to fry,' he drawled in a low, suggestive tone, then with a teasing smile went on: 'During the coming week the press are coming to get all the details, and they want pictures of some of the staff jogging, among other things, so I hope you'll be on hand to give them any information they need.'

'Of course.'

'And from next weekend the Army are making the assault course available for us to get some practice in.'

'I'm afraid I shan't be here,' Valda said rashly.

'Weekend off?' he queried. Valda nodded, beginning to sense that they would soon be back to the usual sparring.

'That's all right,' he continued eagerly, 'if you go home you'll be half way to the Army base as I shall be at Jessica's. I'll pick you up.' He stood up with an air of self-satisfaction.

'I'm sorry, Mr Carr, but I shall be away,' she said, almost catching her breath in anticipation of a change in his mood.

He came to where she was standing between the window and the desk. His nearness unnerved her, sending every resolution of exiling him from her emotions to the four winds. How she simply adored him, and no matter how she tried to show an attitude of abandonment her heart ached with longing for his impetuous style of flirting. He raised his hand, then slowly brought it down on to her shoulder and with a caressing gesture ran it down the length of her arm. She felt as if an electric current had passed through her body. She wanted to step back but she remained mesmerised by the wickedly rakish gleam in his golden eyes.

'That's all right, my dear,' he said with a hidden touch of scorn. 'Have yourself a good break because it'll be the last for six weeks. We've scheduled all the events for mid-August. I expect everyone to be super-fit by then.' He turned and strode off, leaving behind his bigoted aura. He *was* an insufferable bigot, Valda condemned, but his personality was such that it left an indelible imprint wherever he went.

Although Valda was on duty for the weekend it proved to be less stressful than the earlier part of the week. She had just returned from her tea break on Sunday afternoon and was sitting quietly working at her desk as the wards were full of visitors, when a light knock on her half-open door brought a glow of pleasure to her face as she looked up and saw her father standing there.

'Dad!' she greeted, 'Come on in, what are you doing here? Twice in one week!'

'Hallo, love. Come to say I'm sorry I was out when you came home. I was only round at Mary Kepple's.'

He kissed Valda's cheek as she pulled out her visitor's chair for him. 'Mm,' she said mockingly, 'Mary, is it already?'

She thought her father blushed slightly but he raised his finger indignantly. 'Now don't get ideas, Val. I'm only helping out. She doesn't feel too safe yet taking Carlos for walks, so I go along for company. Besides,' he laughed, 'I did enjoy having that little dog to look after, and if I can help Mary why shouldn't I? I haven't got much else to do, and she's a very nice person to be with.'

'I know, Dad, and I agree it's nice for you both to have company.'

'The reason I'm here though is to see young Lee Abbot,' he said seriously.

'Oh, that's nice,' she said sarcastically. 'Never mind about your hard-working daughter.'

'I mind about her a great deal more than I should,' he said with a merry twinkle in his eye. 'I phoned Conifer Lodge when I got home, but they said you were out.'

Valda looked away, somehow feeling unsure of herself.

'Adrian took me out for a meal, it made a nice change,' she said.

'Yes, I must say you look better than when I last saw you.'

'That was a day of days, they happen frequently in hospital.'

'So you'll be off duty all next weekend?' he assumed readily.

'Yes,' Valda hesitantly agreed, 'but Adrian and I are going away for the weekend. We're hoping the weather will stay good. We thought it would be nice to go to the coast. After that, of course, we're all going to be tied up with this fund-raising for the laser machine.'

She tried not to see her father's expression change. It

was only her imagination, she tried to convince herself.

'A decent break will do you good then,' he said, the look on his face not quite in harmony with the words he voiced. 'All the villages round here are holding jumble-sales and fêtes and things for the laser appeal. It's marvellous how people rally together for a good cause.'

'It's all right as long as it doesn't get overdone. People are always being asked to give, but naturally I appreciate the value of the laser machine. It is desperately needed here.'

'Village folk and the townspeople are close, and they like to have a cause to work for. Mr Carr is very popular. People liked the Forbes too so of course everyone is anxious to help.'

'You said you've come to see Lee Abbott. How do you know him, Dad?'

Howard Bergman sighed. 'The family lived in the Addlefield area some years ago. His mother's a bit unstable. Funny thing that, the parents, the old couple, were ordinary decent folk yet the children were all odd. One of the older sons was a bit of an artist and when he was about twenty he took to the road and eventually went off abroad. Then there was another boy who joined up with a circus. We got him back a couple of times while he was under-age but they all had the wanderlust. The older of the two girls went on the stage, chorus girl or something, and only Lee's mother stayed at home. She never married but just got involved with one bloke after another. After the parents died there was a stream of men staying at the house, but there was always too much drinking so fights followed and we used to have to take Lee into care.'

'Deep down Lee's a nice boy. He maintains he wasn't part of either gang that had the fight,' Valda said.

Howard Bergman laughed. 'Innocent bystander—eh? They all say that, but I believe Lee. He's been a loner all his life and never been in any trouble—suppose he

had too much of that when he was a young lad. They
moved away a few years ago. His mother got a living-
in job as a cook-housekeeper on some estate and young
Lee became an apprentice carpenter. Now, I'm interested to know why he came back to this area.'

'He seemed pleased to see you the other day so I'm
sure he'll be glad of someone to talk to.' Valda stood
up, and led the way to room ten. 'I expect he'll be here,
he doesn't seem to mix very well, and so many of them
have gone home this week. There are a lot of new faces,
and he feels embarrassed knowing he's only got a glass
ball in place of one eye.'

Lee was lying on his bed. He seemed to do little else
which Valda knew wasn't the way to prepare for going
home—the difficulty being that he didn't have a home
to go to.

'You've got a visitor, Lee,' she said brightly .

He moved his head slowly and when he saw Howard
he immediately jumped up.

'Sarge!' he greeted, and it did Valda good to hear the
eager response in his voice. 'You're really here to see
blondie I s'pose?'

'No, lad,' Howard said cheerfully. 'I've come especially
to see you.'

Lee inclined his head, the boyish smile fading as
suspicion took its place. 'Police send you?'

Howard laughed . 'No—sit down, Lee, the name's
Howard, I'm not 'Sarge' any longer. How are you
feeling today then?'

Valda slipped unobtrusively away. She returned to
her desk and sat in deep concentration. She knew her
father. He had that special look today, the look which
indicated that he not only cared about his fellow men
but was ready to put himself out to help. Lee was
destined to leave shortly to go to the hostel for young
men. Even if her father only showed an interest, kept
in touch, it would be something.

Valda was right. A few days later when Lee was ready to leave hospital it was Howard Bergman who came in to Addlefield to drive him to the hostel. He helped him settle in, assisted him with claims forms and suchlike, and just before Valda prepared to leave for her weekend with Adrian her father phoned.

'Have a good time, Val, the weather's going to be good just for you. I'm having Lee over for the weekend. Mary's coming here for a meal, and then we're going over to her place for the day on Sunday. Look forward to seeing you when you get back, love,' and he rang off.

Suddenly he had become a very busy man and Valda smiled secretly. Sebastian had accused her of helping lame ducks but now her father had taken them on. They couldn't be in better hands and at least it might prevent her father from brooding about her and Adrian going off for the weekend.

They set off soon after seven o'clock on Friday evening in high spirits.

'You haven't told me where we're going,' Valda said.

'The coast, Burnham-on-Sea actually. I know we aren't likely to see the sea too often on that particular coast but a weekend isn't long enough to travel far. In this heat we don't want to spend hours driving. We must make up our minds to go abroad somewhere. Where d'you fancy?' Adrian asked, glancing across at Valda.

'What a question,' she said. 'Everywhere—anywhere, I should think. I don't really fancy the real tourist spots around Spain though, too crowded.'

'Somewhere exotic I suppose, like Tunisia or Cyprus?'

'Mm, why not? Like I said, anywhere really.'

'We must pick up some brochures when we get back and make up our minds.'

If Valda was surprised at Adrian's suggestion she didn't show it. They'd often talked in the past of doing things which somehow never quite came off. She had to pinch herself to believe that this weekend was actually happening. Surely it was just a dream and in a minute she would wake up and find herself back at Addlefield Eye Hospital, but it was real enough.

They took the journey at a medium pace and as the evening wore on the traffic became lighter. It was about nine o'clock when Adrian drove up in front of a rather elegant hotel.

'Golly, I thought you were going to take me to some isolated hide-away,' Valda said in surprise.

'Our room will be just as isolated as a deserted cove miles from anywhere, probably more so, darling. We're far less likely to be ogled at a place like this than in a small village.'

'Why might we be ogled?' she asked with a grin.

'Because we're going to register as Adrian Wallace and Valda Bergman,' he answered confidently. 'No, Valda, this isn't a cunning way of getting you into my bed. There's always a welcome for you there, that goes without saying, but I want this to be a special time when we can forget patients and colleagues, and devote our time to one another.'

Valda dropped her gaze. She knew he was thinking mainly of her father, and she knew too that this idea was an excellent one—or would have been if a certain consultant didn't invade her private thoughts far too frequently.

'Don't worry, darling,' Adrian assured her, misconstruing her silence. 'Hotels this size don't question who shares a room, and it is a twin-bedded room incidentally —en-suite, of course.'

When they reached the sea-front hotel, to anyone watching they were just an ordinary couple in love who signed the hotel register and walked hand in hand to the lift where a porter waited with their cases.

Room thirteen was on the first floor, a spacious luxurious room with a small balcony overlooking a large swimming-pool. They settled in and unpacked and after a meal they sat on the terrace to enjoy a drink.

Valda began to feel some apprehension as bedtime approached but alone in their room all her fears drifted away. Adrian clasped her to him and his kisses became impulsive so that when Valda closed her eyes it was easy to imagine that it was Sebastian who was holding her and loving her.

'Just to prove how much I love you, Val, and to show you that it isn't a ploy on my part to do all that I'm sorely tempted to do, I promise I shall stay in my own bed—until you suggest otherwise, that is,' Adrian said, holding her away from him for a moment.

Valda slipped her arms around his neck and drew his face down to hers.

'You are nice,' she crooned to him. 'That's what I call being understanding—after all, this is quite a new experience for me. I'm not in the habit of sharing a room with an unmarried man.'

'Nor a married one, I hope,' Adrian said quickly, then with a grin added, 'Neither have I had the pleasure with young ladies of hitherto good character.' He looked down into her face and pecked the tip of her nose. 'What does your father think of this idea then?'

'He thought it was a good one—us coming together, I mean. Oh, I'm sure he disapproves in his paternal way, but I am over eighteen, even twenty-one,' she giggled.

Adrian held on to her in a tender but possessive way. He looked thoughtful, doubtful even, and she gazed at him with a worried frown creasing her brow.

'What's the matter, Adrian? You look as if something's wrong.'

Could he actually be nervous? she wondered, aware of his heart thudding against her breast.

'Don't you know, darling?' he whispered.

'No—what could possibly be wrong?' she asked with genuine concern.

'Oh, sweetheart, this is the hardest thing a man ever

has to do, and I'm so *terrified*.' And yet he was smiling, laughing even, albeit a nervous laugh. 'I love you, Valda darling, and I want you to say "yes", but I'm afraid you'll say "no"—but I *do* want us to be married.'

Married! The idea was such a shock that Valda was unable to respond. Wasn't this the moment that she had longed for, dreamed of? And yet here she was riveted to the spot and completely tongue-tied.

Finally she let a laugh of relief escape her lips and she drew Adrian's head down to kiss him forcefully.

'I thought you'd never ask,' she whispered affectionately.

'Then it's—yes? Oh, darling—' He drew her against him in a bear-hug, so tight in fact that her feet left the floor as he whizzed her round in a frenzy of delight.

'We'll buy the ring tomorrow,' he promised urgently.

'I thought we came to swim,' Valda said feeling decidedly light-headed.

'We're going to swim through the rest of our days together, darling.'

Adrian forced her backwards on to the nearest bed. His lips were tender on hers and his fingers gentle as he explored the delectable curves of her relaxed body. The room seemed to be going round and round somewhere high above her while she waited eagerly for her lover to arouse the passion that lay inert deep inside her, but instead of inducing her sexual instincts he caressed and soothed until she dreamily slipped into a heavy slumber . . .

The remainder of the weekend seemed unreal to Valda. Not that she didn't enjoy it, and purchasing the ring was the highlight as with Adrian's help she selected one—a golden topaz centre stone with shoulders encrusted with small turquoise and diamonds. On Valda's slim, elegant finger it looked magnificent, the large oval stone sparkling up at her like an eye winking mischievously.

All too soon it came to an end and reality returned, and Valda became more sombre as they neared familiar landmarks. Going off with Adrian for a weekend had been a wild, glorious intermission. Becoming engaged and vowing to love Adrian had even been easy so many miles from everyone they knew. What had she done? Committed herself to something which didn't seem to glitter quite as much as they sped back to commonplace suroundings.

CHAPTER NINE

'So, it was *that* kind of weekend, was it?' Howard Bergman's voice boomed down the telephone line into Valda's ear.

Adrian had driven to Maple Cottage only to find it empty. They had let themselves in with Valda's key, made coffee and waited nervously, but when Valda's father hadn't shown up by ten o'clock they left again. Valda remembered that he and Lee were going to spend the day with Miss Kepple.

Now, the following day, it was Valda's lunch break and she had walked to a telephone kiosk near the Jester inn to phone her father and give him the news. Pay phones at Conifer Lodge and the hospital were too public for what she had to say.

'No!' she answered back sharply, 'it wasn't *that* kind of weekend.' Her cheeks were crimson at her father's inference, and that her news vexed him she had no doubt by his tone.

There was a prolonged silence before her father said, 'Then it ought to have been—that's if you're really in love,' he challenged, his voice a shade contrite, with a hint of humour for good measure.

Valda sighed impatiently. 'There's no pleasing you, is there?' she said crossly.

The familiar chuckle did nothing to appease her.

'I wouldn't expect you to admit to what kind of weekend you had, love,' he said, 'but if you say it was all purity and innocence then I believe you, and if marrying Adrian is what you want then you know you have my blessing.'

'I know it must have come as a shock,' Valda went

on. 'Adrian just—swept me off my feet.' She hoped that she had successfully hidden the break in her voice. 'But I do want you to be pleased, Dad.'

'Of course I'm happy for you, my dear. Can't think what's been keeping that young man. So you've got the ring and everything's all set for a shot-gun wedding?' Howard Bergman laughed heartily. 'I don't really mean that, I'm only teasing,' he added.

'We're engaged, and Adrian's bought me a lovely ring. We haven't planned any further ahead than that as yet,' Valda explained. 'How did your weekend go?'

'Splendid. Lee seemed to enjoy being with us old cronies—we might just be able to help him over these next few awkward weeks.'

'I'll try and come home soon, Dad,' she said, expecting the pips to go at any minute.

'Mary's got her appointment at the ophthalmic clinic later this week. We'll take you out to lunch if you can spare a couple of hours. Perhaps Adrian could join us. Have a little family celebration.'

'That would be nice,' she agreed. 'See you, Dad,' and she rang off as the pips echoed loudly. So Mary Kepple had become 'family' in double-quick time.

She walked briskly back to the hospital, and had time for coffee and a cheese roll before returning to duty. She was thankful to have got that over with. Her father had accepted her news reasonably calmly. Now it could become common knowledge. She supposed she ought to have shouted it from the rooftops, but as yet she hadn't had the opportunity or desire to confide in anyone.

It was quite early next morning when Sebastian Carr arrived to visit his patients and he came with his retinue of housemen and registrar. For once he was doing what one would expect of a consultant, Valda thought, as Nurse Dickson called her from the main ward where she had been attending to an elderly female patient who suffered from a heart condition, and from the report

Valda learned she had been restless overnight with breathing difficulties.

Valda went at once to her office and found Sebastian in discussion with his team. Registrar and housemen wore white coats but Sebastian was wearing a dark blue suit with a narrow pin-stripe, and as always looked distinguished.

'Good morning,' Valda greeted to no one in particular and immediately Sebastian swung round.

'Ah, Sister, I believe congratulations are in order?'

Valda felt her eyes smarting under his scrutiny, and she guessed that her father must be the culprit.

'Thank you, Mr Carr,' she replied demurely, hoping that he would not pursue the matter, but Sebastian had other ideas.

'Oh, I know it's not correct to congratulate you on catching your man. It's Adrian who must be congratulated, but perhaps I'm permitted to kiss the charming bride-to-be instead.'

One moment he seemed coldly remote, the next he had spanned the distance between them, and holding her gently had placed his lips very firmly against hers.

She felt as if she were trapped in a cauldron of fire, and as she dared to meet his gaze she saw the wicked gleam in his golden blandishing eyes. He picked up her left hand and caressed her naked fourth finger while he probed between the top and second button of her dress with the fingers of his other hand.

'You see how well-informed I am?' he said smoothly as he exposed the ring still attached to its gold chain round her neck. He held it between his two fingers and she hated him for humiliating her in front of his colleagues. She couldn't look down at the ring for many seconds without going cross-eyed as the chain wasn't long enough, so there was simply nowhere else to look except into his face. She had likened the oval topaz stone to a mischievous eye, and now she had no doubt as to whose eyes it reminded her of.

'I hope Adrian will make you very happy,' he whispered as if he didn't intend the others to hear, then he added in a more prominent voice, 'I'm sure we all wish you the very best for the future, Sister.' He half-turned to the grinning Ray Pyke and Duncan Fraser. 'Kissing the bride-to-be is a special privilege accorded to consultants only,' and without warning he pressed his lips to hers again.

Valda felt utterly defeated, and much too self-conscious to remonstrate with him as she checked that her cap was still in place on her head. She tucked her ring back inside her dress again, straightened her apron and gathered up a handful of folders from her desk.

Why did his devastating kisses linger on her lips? Why couldn't she see him for what he was? Even as she led the way back into the ward she was conscious of his compelling magnetism. Adrian was sweet and tender in his wooing, so much so that he had lulled her to sleep, but just one kiss from Sebastian Carr and she knew her heart was rapping out a warning, a signal of dangerous disquiet.

Somehow she escorted the doctors through the unit, giving them the information they required, answering when questions were put to her and almost sighing with relief when they finally departed.

Thank God she was working a split shift. Noon couldn't come fast enough. She didn't bother with a meal—how could she eat when the enormity of her deception hammered in her brain? In the quietness of her room at Conifer Lodge she censured herself for her insincerity. Her father was right as always. She didn't *love* Adrian, not the way she did Sebastian. It was cruel and it hurt. She even tried to ridicule herself out of such an admission. The consultant taunted, made fun of her. How could you love a man who did that? But she did, hopelessly, helplessly—and uselessly. He couldn't possibly love her or he wouldn't humiliate her like he did—of course, she thought miserably, there was

Miranda. Wasn't *she* the lucky one! Valda knew she was being unforgivably disloyal to Adrian. She ought to feel radiant, eager to share her happy news with everyone she met, but reservations were piling one on top of another. She tried to see herself as the wife of a general practitioner, but somehow she simply didn't fit the bill. She had no idea why—she was far less suited to being a consultant's wife! Miranda was so frightfully young but she did have a certain way with her. Self-confidence, Valda assumed it must be, and she was steeped in gloom as she confessed that it was the one thing she lacked.

Then she shook herself out of such gloom. She had reached an important point in her life. Miranda couldn't be allowed to have all the luck. Adrian was attractive and he was her fiancé at last so she had nothing to feel downcast about. She went off to the end of the passageway and enjoyed a warm shower, at the same time washing her hair, and by the time she returned to the eye wards after a cup of tea in the Sisters' lounge at Conifer Lodge she felt more in control of herself. There was only one thing to do and that was make the best of the situation. She and Adrian would do all right together with a large slice of luck.

The news had spread like wildfire. When Valda reached her office she found a huge bouquet of flowers on her desk and from the loving message on the card discovered that they were from Adrian. There were one or two envelopes containing congratulatory cards from various members of the staff on her unit. They gathered round, begging to see her ring, and it seemed that every few minutes colleagues came from other wards and departments to share in her happiness.

Eventually peace reigned throughout the eye unit but it was later than usual when Valda sat down to write her report. She closed the door in the hope that no one would disturb her and became so engrossed in her job that she got through it quickly, which was just as well because Pam Gardner arrived early, bearing a suspicious looking bottle wrapped in tissue paper.

'Val—I'm so pleased for you,' she greeted warmly. 'Here, I thought we could all have a little drink to celebrate. I've no doubt everyone will be assembling at the Jester later tonight but us night staff always miss the parties so we'll have our own.'

'We'll all get shot,' Valda laughed, 'but it is a special occasion.'

'I met the SNO and for once she approved, but said she'd better not come up; she'd do her best to keep everyone else away.'

Valda called all the staff into her office and they drank a toast to the newly engaged couple. It was a bit of a hen party which didn't last long as there were last minute jobs to do while Valda gave her report to Pam. They were just completing the details of new admissions ready for the theatre list the next day when the door opened and Sebastian Carr walked in. He took in the scene at a glance and managed a smile which didn't reach his eyes even though, with a nod towards the empty sherry bottle he said, 'I see I'm too late to join in the celebrations.'

'We did have permission, sir,' Pam excused hurriedly. 'Night staff tend to get left out and I'm sure you'll want to congratulate Sister Bergman.'

'I've already done so,' he said quietly. 'In fact I rather think I helped to publicise the event. Our delectable Nordic beauty has suddenly gone shy on us.' There was a cynical twist to his mouth as he looked from Valda back to Pam. 'It's Sister Bergman I came to see, Sister Gardner.'

'Of course, sir, I've plenty to do.' Pam took the hint and left the office, taking care to close the door tightly.

Sebastian picked up the cards from the desk and eyed the bouquet with some amusement, which irritated Valda.

'Thank you for feeding the grapevine,' she said stonily.

'I presume you heard it from my father?'

'No, Valda, actually I heard the exciting news from Merle. I would rather have heard it from you.' His tone had changed to a mixture of sarcasm and contempt.

'I'm very sorry,' Valda said heatedly with equally as much sarcasm. 'If I'd known I'd have phoned you from Burnham-on-Sea!'

'Don't try to be smart, young lady. I suppose all this has been neatly arranged so that you think you can wriggle out of helping with the fund-raising? When's the wedding—next week?'

'Of course not,' Valda snapped.

'It had better not be.' He put both hands on the desk and leaned towards her. 'So, how was the weekend? Plenty of physical exercise, I hope?'

'It wasn't like that,' she said, her cheeks flushing dark red.

Sebastian laughed and stood back, digging his hands deep into pockets. 'What other way is there?' he asked pointedly. 'What was it, Jones? Smith? Brown? Black?'

'Wallace and Bergman,' she retorted obstinately.

He walked to the window so that he was standing with his back to her. 'How delightfully naïve,' he muttered darkly, then he strode back to where she was standing at the desk. '*I* know just what makes you tick, Valda, and I find what you suggest hard to believe. You've managed to persuade him to give you a ring, but for God's sake keep it round your neck so that *I* can't see it. For as long as my crusade lasts I want you *uncommitted*, and don't you forget *that*!'

'What I do with my own time is *my* affair,' Valda yelled at him, hot and furious. 'How can *my* engagement to Adrian affect *your* blasted crusade?'

He gripped her shoulders and shook her roughly.

'It's *our* crusade, damn you! You're part of it whether you like it or not. So you dislike me and my ideas, but we're both dedicated to a cause, and you'd better save all the passion until after we've got the laser machine

—which I mean to have at *all* costs!'

'It doesn't only depend on me,' she argued violently. 'There's a whole hospital full of people who are only too willing to help you get the money you need. Why pick on me?'

He pulled her up against him with such force that their knees collided.

'Because—' but he didn't finish. The flashing anger in his eyes smouldered, and she knew it was useless to try to avoid his lips claiming her mouth which was all too ready to respond.

Although she was burning with indignation, she could feel his ardour bursting within him. She tried to gasp for breath but his mouth savaged hers until she was too weak to protest.

'That's why I picked on you—*that's* what there is between us, and when you're lying in Adrian's arms at night remember who you're committed to,' he growled.

He flung her from him and she staggered back into her chair. It was a few minutes before she could find her voice, then she stood up once more to resume the verbal battle.

'I'm certainly not committed to *you*,' she stressed adamantly, 'and as to lying in Adrian's arms at night—for heaven's sake, we've only just got engaged! Adrian has his flat, I have my room at Conifer Lodge. Just because we enjoy a weekend away doesn't mean we have to shack up together.'

'No?' He turned and sneered. 'I thought everyone these days went in for trial marriages. You're a tease—you want fulfilment, but it has to be on your terms. Women are all the same, it's all take and no give. Well, just don't go wearing yourself out, sweetheart, because I've got your name on half a dozen sponsorship forms. You've got to set an example, and—' he smiled triumphantly, 'lots of your ex-patients seem only too delighted to sponsor you in the various events.'

'You—you—!' she couldn't find anything abusive

enough to call him. 'You had no right,' she managed lamely.

He started towards her again and she promptly sat down, deciding that was the safest option. He stretched out his hand and curled his slender fingers round her chin, holding her fast.

'I have every right. You've been quite an athlete in the past so now's your chance to show me what stimulates that intense sexual drive of yours.'

'Huh!' Valda snorted angrily. 'You don't know the first thing about my sexual drive. You're the tease,' she accused. 'You're the one who thinks you can get what you want by—by . . .'

'Go on?' he urged provocatively.

'By taking liberties,' she finally alleged.

He had the audacity to tickle her chin at which she smacked his hand sharply, and goaded him with her militant expression.

Sebastian merely laughed, spurred on by the blazing malice in her eyes.

'Go on, fight me,' he tormented as he brushed her cheeks with first his left hand, then his right. His movements were light and playful as he danced from one foot to the other teasing her in earnest. She pushed her chair back in an effort to avoid him, but he followed, and as she stood up he caught her in a dance hold and waltzed her round the office, ending the fun and games with a meaningful kiss.

Valda stamped her foot in temper. 'Stop it!' she cried, outraged. 'I hate you!'

'Ah,' he said, inclining his head and lifting a warning finger towards her. 'You wish you did. The battle is on, my Nordic beauty—may the best man win.' He released her and walked to the door. 'We have a great deal to do, my dear—you especially, to get fit. Loving and hating are splendid exercises, but don't neglect the more practical methods.' He waved chivalrously from the open doorway. 'Have a good party.'

Valda could have wept, but she was too mad. He was everything that he accused her of being. Party indeed! She had never felt less partyish, but she had to show willing she supposed so she tidied her desk, said goodnight to the night staff and went to Conifer Lodge. The time was getting on so she had a quick freshen-up, let her hair down, put on a simple floral summer dress and cardigan and walked down the road to the inn.

It didn't seem right to be celebrating without Adrian, but although she dialled his flat number a few times there was no reply. He was probably at the club, and when a niggling voice suggested he might be with Merle she dismissed it from her mind quickly. She could always try Merle's number, of course, but no way was she going to admit that she didn't actually know where Adrian was.

In spite of herself, and although the celebrations seemed somewhat misguided, Valda's colleagues saw to it that she enjoyed herself, and it was quite a noisy brigade of off-duty nursing staff who wended their way back to the hospital shortly before midnight. The evening had ended with general discussion about the enthusiasm of Sebastian Carr and his crusade, and Valda's last thoughts before sleeping were concerned with what events the consultant had put her name down for. She giggled now at his comment about her intense sexual drive; she only wished Adrian's were the same. Was she really prepared to go into marriage knowing that another man was capable of arousing her to ecstasy so much more skilfully than her fiancé?

As the days passed Valda felt she was living two separate lives. When she was with Adrian she had few doubts about their future together; when she was at work, just to hear Sebastian's voice filled her with fearful misgivings.

She managed to have a half-day off when Miss

Kepple attended the ophthalmic clinic for a check-up, and she enjoyed accompanying Mary and her father for lunch in the restaurant of one of the more regal hotels in Addlefield. Adrian was able to join them too and it proved to be a happy occasion.

Valda quickly jumped to conclusions. She wasn't jealous, but it became obvious that Mary Kepple was becoming important to her father. So, in her off-duty periods Valda didn't have to phone him, or rush home to Maple Cottage at every opportunity. Instead she involved herself in a hard training scheme in readiness for the events of the crusade. Just to outwit Sebastian, though, she kept it all very much to herself, and instead of joining the early morning jogging team she did her own thing in her own time.

The local comprehensive school made one of their two ultra-modern gymnasiums available for the hospital staff and Valda occasionally went there with Pam Gardner for a good work-out session, but mostly she ran alone and in the evenings. She would drive away from the hospital in her car and then run along lonely country lanes where she was unlikely to meet anyone she knew. The running track at the school was helpful too for getting her back to the capabilities she'd had at school. She guessed that her father had told Sebastian Carr that during the last two years at the local grammar school Valda had won cups and medals for running. She'd been good at most sports except swimming, and now, as the weeks flew by she enjoyed the challenge and admitted that she was feeling in good form.

Sebastian insisted on weekly committee meetings, but in the main these were an occasion for him to keep his helpers informed of the progress that his crusade was making, and there was no denying that he knew the road to success. A great deal of publicity by local radio and the press had already helped to swell the target thermometer and such were his efforts that he seemed to have given up tormenting Valda. For her part she kept out of his way as much as possible. Speculative rumours were running rife on the grapevine about the gorgeous black-haired girl, whom Valda guessed must be Miranda, who shadowed him wherever he went, and was usually accompanied by the sleek-coated Great Dane.

'Love me, love my dog,' Valda thought and guessed that Sebastian's wife would need to have passed a dog-lover's test before he would pop the question. That, she assumed, he had already done as he had gone as far as having a property built, and that the lovely Miranda was acceptable in every way was apparent.

Valda met her one evening as she was walking to the pub to meet Adrian. As Valda rounded a corner in the lane an enormous creature leapt at her from a field gate. He put his giant paws up on Valda's shoulders and tried to lick her face in greeting.

'Get down, Misty,' Miranda commanded. 'Oh, hallo,' she went on when she recognised Valda. 'He goes a bundle on you, doesn't he? His master would not be pleased to see I've got him off the lead so don't tell your boss, will you?'

'Of course not,' Valda agreed, trying to keep the animal at bay.'He's a handful though, I should think.'

'Seb's very firm with him. He thinks I'm too easy, but a dog this size needs lots of space, that's why I have him at my place through the week. I've just cut across that field. I've walked miles in the hope that Misty will be tired out by the time Seb gets to his flat. I hope he hasn't made your suit all dirty. You always look so smart, Valda. I envy you your colouring. Men always prefer blondes.'

Valda laughed. 'It isn't only blondes who find husbands,' she said.

'But you've found yours. Gosh, you are lucky. Adrian is *so* handsome. Are you off to meet him now?'

Valda nodded. 'That's right, so if you'll excuse me—we get so little time together.'

Miranda attached Misty's lead to his collar and the girls went their separate ways. Valda was surprised at Miranda's admiration of Adrian, but then, didn't everyone admire Adrian's good looks and impeccable manners. But why couldn't Miranda be grateful for what she'd got? She was a raven-haired beauty with perfect skin and she had attracted the most desirable of men in Valda's eyes. He was desirable, but far from perfect. Perhaps that was what was wrong. Maybe it was Sebastian's devilish moods which she found irresistible whereas Adrian was just a little too good. But it was the perfect gallantry with which he greeted her as Valda went straight into the lounge bar which helped her to forget Sebastian for the time being.

Adrian stood up, kissed Valda dutifully, then waited until she was seated before he went to the bar to fetch her usual schooner of sweet sherry. When he returned he put his arm round her shoulders possessively, and they were lost to the rest of the pub's clientele.

Valda walked her fingers up his tanned arms. 'You're a super colour,' she said, then with a mischievous twinkle added, 'Don't tell me, I know, it's the benefits of the club.'

'Am I getting through to you at last? Actually, darling, I appreciate that you haven't really the time to make use of a full membership. Not at present. It would be better in the winter, but who knows where we'll be by then?' He planted a resounding kiss on her cheek.

'Still in Addlefield doing the same old routine,' Valda told him drily.

Adrian sipped his drink. 'Perhaps not, Val. I've been thinking—well, it's only a thought as yet, but when we get married let's move away from here? But there's your father,' he added doubtfully.

Valda twirled her glass between dainty fingers. The stones on her engagement ring caught the light and gleamed brilliantly. She hastily turned it round so that she couldn't see that eye blinking at her.

'Dad isn't a problem,' she said rashly. 'He's always said he'd never stand in my way if I wanted to go away to work so he wouldn't—he can't say anything once we're married.'

'Abroad perhaps?' Adrian suggested.

'Anywhere special in mind?'

'Somewhere with a good climate—somewhere with better prospects.'

'But you've got a job, darling,' Valda said. 'That counts for quite a lot these days, and what's wrong with Addlefield anyway?'

Adrian pursed his lips. 'Nothing, except that I don't fancy married life with my father-in-law breathing down my neck.'

'Dad isn't like that,' Valda defended swiftly, 'and now there seems to be Mary Kepple who might be hankering after becoming Mrs Bergman.'

'Would you mind?'

It was Valda's turn to compress her lips. 'Mm . . . things wouldn't be quite the same, would they?'

'They won't anyway when we get married. I like Miss Kepple, and I really think she and your dad are very well-suited, but I fancy having you somewhere all to myself.'

'We're in a crowded room now, but you've got me all to yourself,' Valda said seductively, smiling at him.

He raised his eyebrows. 'Have I?' he asked gently.

Valda looked away quickly. Something in his expression warned her against questioning his doubt, but in spite of the warning she asked, 'Who else is intruding?'

'I wish I knew.'

'You're being mysterious,' Valda accused.

'That should make me more intriguing then.' He pulled her against him. 'Sometimes I feel that you're not quite real.'

Valda giggled and ran her fingers down his thigh. She knew that he liked her to fondle him.

'Don't pinch me to find out,' she whispered. 'I'm real enough.'

'That's what I keep telling myself,' he replied and nibbled her ear.

Just before closing time they left the haven of intimacy and wandered in close harmony back to Conifer Lodge.

'I'm going away on a week's course soon but after that we'll make some definite arrangements,' Adrian said. 'I'll see what jobs are available and we'll take it from there. We can still set the wedding date—when you've consulted your diary, then we can visit my parents in London for a weekend.'

Valda agreed to all his suggestions, but as soon as she was alone she began to question everything. Doubts refused to be swept aside and yet she allowed herself to dream about a future with Adrian.

It would be best she told herself. Much more sensible to go away and start their married life afresh, where there was no Sebastian and Miranda to envy, no Merle to feel uneasy about, and no Miss Kepple to be jealous of. She experienced a cold shiver when she thought about the ordeal of meeting Adrian's family. They were business people, his two brothers involved in the family partnership. Only Adrian was the odd one out. Perhaps they wouldn't like her. Even though her father was being terribly nice about it all Valda was aware of his regrets, but she didn't understand them. Adrian was a qualified doctor with a faultless reputation, and extra good looks as a bonus, but what would the Wallaces think of their son marrying a girl whose father was a divorced, retired police-sergeant? Money breeds money, Valda remembered her father saying, so she doubted that her humble background would be good enough for them. Now Merle Decarta might be more in the correct league for Adrian, Valda realised, but it wasn't Merle's finger that Adrian had adorned with a ring. It was hers. She looked down at the resplendent topaz and it was just as if Sebastian Carr was mocking her again. But he didn't mock her any more. He'd tired of that game. His crusade was all that mattered to him now and as everyone was being so helpful he had no need of Valda.

It occurred to her that he might have become reconciled to the fact that she and Adrian were serious in their intention to get married so he was doing the honourable thing and letting them get on with it. This made Valda feel more desolate than ever. She would *hate* to leave Addlefield. It would be hell to go on nursing for the rest of her days, knowing that he was living with the slightly crazy Miranda in a spectacular new house; coming into contact with him almost daily in a professional way and yet loving him just too, *too* much. It would be hell, but she'd revel in every minute of her misery. No, she was going to marry Adrian—why let Merle have her handsome fiancé? And they were going to move away into the unknown.

What else could she do? She reproached herself daily for being weak, selfish, and so indecisive. She was trying to get the best of both worlds and she was in danger of losing everything. If she married Adrian how could they be happy? He would soon discover that her heart wasn't truly his. Didn't he know that already? Hadn't he said that she wasn't quite real to him? If only she had the courage to be as honest as her heart wanted to be!

Yet, in spite of the hours she spent trying to sort out her conflicting thoughts she became closer in many ways to Adrian. She was trying to make up to him for the mean trick she was playing on him, knowing that sooner or later she was going to let him down. She was glad she had to spend much of her free time preparing for the events. It prevented her from seeing too much of her father for she felt sure he would take one look at her and know that she was in a great quandary. It also kept her and Adrian apart, though when he could, he accompanied her to the school gym, and even ran with her some evenings.

Sebastian didn't bother her at all. She didn't care

whether he knew that she was training hard or not. No doubt Merle was keeping him well-informed of all that passed between herself and Adrian, and she felt an increasing urge to find Sebastian and tell him the truth. She knew she never would, of course, because for one thing she would hate to come between him and Miranda, so being engaged to Adrian was rather like being protected by a safety net.

CHAPTER TEN

ADRIAN went away on his course and although Valda endeavoured to keep occupied, the fact that her personal love-life was being torn in two different ways caused her nothing but unhappiness.

The misery grew until she admitted defeat. Her father had always been her closest friend so what could it matter if he did say 'I told you so'.

She decided to go home on her half-day off and talk things over with him, but as she drew up at the five-barred gate Carlos came yapping from the back garden.

Her father usually came to help her with the gate but not today; she reached the back door before she heard his voice calling: 'Come on in, love, we can do with an extra pair of hands.'

There was a strong, sweet smell wafting from the window, and as soon as Valda entered the kitchen she realised that Mary Kepple and her father were busy making jam.

The contents of an outsized preserving pan were spitting fractiously and Mary Kepple, flushed but smiling, turned to greet Valda.

'Hallo, my dear, how nice to see you.'

'You're busy I see,' Valda observed, noting the water-proof apron Miss Kepple was wearing and the scarf protecting her hair, as well as the blue and white butcher's apron her father had on. The scene was one of domestic disruptive harmony!

'Gooseberry and strawberry,' her father briefed, stopping to kiss her cheek before continuing to dry the jam jars and put them to warm.

Mary Kepple waved the wooden spoon towards him.

'You go and sit down with Valda and enjoy a chat, Howard. I'll see to the jam.'

'Oh no,' Howard said. 'We started this together so we'll finish it together. Val, you're just in time to make us a cup of tea.'

Valda was grateful for the tea and when the jam was ready she helped to get it potted and labelled.

'I had the strawberries in my freezer but they don't keep too well in there,' Mary explained, 'so your Dad and I picked some gooseberries up at Home Farm and decided the jam would go down a treat at the Summer Fayre. All the proceeds are going to the laser appeal this year. Isn't that good?'

Valda agreed that it was, but oh how she needed to talk to her father alone. It was not to be. Howard and Mary were off to Deasley village hall to play Bingo in aid of—what else but the laser appeal!

'You could come too, love,' her father urged. 'I expect you're missing Adrian. Come and have a laugh with the locals. Your Mr Carr is coming to chair the proceedings and we shall go for a drink before I take Mary home.'

'I . . . I've got things to do, Dad, and I'm on early shift tomorrow. I'll be home for the weekend though. Adrian won't get back until Monday as he's visiting his parents while he's in London.'

Her father met her gaze with an apologetic smile.

'I've promised to take Lee to see the charity cricket match on Saturday, and on Sunday we're going to see his mother near Bristol. Naturally, I thought—'

'You don't have to alter your plans for me,' Valda said quickly. 'I'm glad you're helping Lee. I expect I shall find some odd jobs here that need doing.'

'I thought you'd be busy training,' Howard said.

'I am, of course, who isn't? But I can still go for a run from here.'

'How about coming over to see me on Sunday, Valda dear? Saturday too if you like?' Mary Kepple invited.

'That's very kind of you,' Valda began, trying to

come up with an excuse to refuse, but how could she without appearing ungracious? 'All right, Sunday then?' she agreed.

Somehow over the weekend she would find a moment to talk to her father alone, she thought, but Lee spent all day Saturday with them, staying overnight so that they could make an early start to Bristol next morning.

There had been a break in the weather. It was dull and often showery but after her father and Lee had set off on Sunday morning Valda went for a run round the lanes which were so familiar to her. No way could she imagine herself confiding in Mary Kepple, but when Valda reached the cottage on Deasley Common she was greeted so warmly and made to feel so relaxed that she found herself chattering easily to Miss Kepple over afternoon tea. Not about the things that lay so heavy on her heart, but about Lee, and afterwards the local people whom they both knew.

Valda offered to wash up.

'No, my dear. You work quite hard enough. This is your weekend off and you must relax. You don't look too well, you know. Let's leave the tea things and just sit and chat. It's a pity the weather's so changeable, let's hope it improves for the day when all the events are to take place. Now you will bring me your sponsorship form to sign, won't you?'

Valda's mind had gone off in other directions again but she rallied when she realised that Miss Kepple was speaking.

'You have a lovely home, Miss Kepple,' she said and truly meant it. The cottage was modernised yet had been furnished with good solid furniture, antique reproductions, Valda guessed.

'I love my home, dear,' Miss Kepple said, 'and you really must stop calling me Miss Kepple.'

Valda dropped her gaze into her lap. If her father married this woman what was she going to call her then?

'Valda dear—we must be honest with each other. I
believe I can understand what unhappiness you're going
through just now, but first if a little plain speaking will
put your mind at rest on one score maybe you'll be able
to unravel your other troubles more easily.'

Valda looked up quickly, alert and suddenly on the
defensive.

'I know you're unhappy, Valda,' Mary Kepple went
on, 'but if you're anticipating a future stepmother, then
let me tell you that Howard and I are happy to go on
being good friends, and wholly independent.'

'But . . . but, Miss—'

'Mary.'

Valda smiled. 'Mary—I wouldn't have minded,
honestly. In fact I think Dad must be more lonely than
he ever lets on, but I didn't suggest he took Carlos
because—I mean I never intended to play Cupid.'

Miss Kepple reciprocated with a much more generous
smile. 'I'm quite sure you didn't. You have too much
to worry about on your own account.'

Valda was tempted to demand what Mary Kepple
knew, but she hesitated, her brow puckered quizzically.

'I wanted Howard to tell you that while we've grown
fond of each other we've decided to remain as we are.
He seemed to think that if you took the hint of us
getting together it might help you to go ahead with
your own plans. Men can be blind sometimes though,
can't they?'

'What do you mean, Mary?' Valda asked gently.

'You aren't really in love with Adrian, are you?'

'Dad isn't so blind then, is he?' Valda replied, unable
to bear the older woman's scrutiny.

'Your father felt something wasn't quite right, but *I*
know it's because you love Sebastian Carr.'

Valda almost jumped up, but managed to remain on
the edge of her chair.

Mary shook her head slowly. 'Valda dear, it can be
our secret. I haven't voiced my opinion to your father,

nor do I intend to. I only want you to know that I understand completely.'

'Do you?' Valda muttered. 'How can anyone? I had no idea it showed.'

'Pain is usually reflected in one's eyes, but perhaps I can see it more clearly than others because I was once in a similar position. I gave my ring back to the man I was cheating, and I silently loved from afar a man who didn't even notice me.'

Valda leaned forward and placed her hand over Mary's.

'Mary,' she breathed. 'You threw away your chances of even companionship?'

'Oh, Valda—that might be good enough for the over sixties but not for the young, and I was round about your age.'

'Are you telling me I should give Adrian back his ring?'

'I'm not telling you anything. Just do what you know will be right.'

'But he'll take it badly. He'll be so hurt and after so short a time.'

'That's a risk you'll have to take. Perhaps not as much as you think. My Bill was outraged, threatened suicide, but within a year he'd married someone else. Men are unpredictable. I know you want to spare him, but I advise you to think carefully. Better no marriage at all than an unhappy one. You'll get over it. Just don't worry about what others may think, it's *your* life—and Sebastian's.'

'If only that were true,' Valda sighed. 'We've got our own lives—yes—but he doesn't care for me, not in that way. His crusade is all that matters to him, and besides he already has his woman, and marriage can't be far away as he's having a house built.' Valda stared out of the window deep in thought. 'Mary,' she said, turning suddenly, 'you have been a help, at least it's sorted out one problem—that's if I can find the courage to do what I've known all along I ought to do—and if you and Dad ever change your mind you'll make a super step-mum.'

'Valda,' Mary Kepple's eyes misted over and her chin trembled, 'if I'd had a daughter of my own I would like her to have been just like you.'

Valda wrinkled her nose and made a grotesque expression as she laughed. 'That's what they mean by looking through rose-coloured spectacles. Right now I don't like myself very much. As Dad will tell you, I can be as stubborn as a mule.'

'But you're like him with a loving and tender heart.'

Valda had to concentrate hard as she drove back to Conifer Lodge on the wet roads. One half of her wished that Adrian was returning to Addlefield tonight so that she could get it over and done with; the other half of her dreaded their meeting and Adrian's reaction, but she plucked up enough courage when she went off duty next day to ring the Health Centre.

She asked for Adrian and immediately the female at the other end of the line recognised her voice.

'Valda, isn't it? Merle here. Adrian's still out on his round, I'm afraid. He got back last night after all. He went to Maple Cottage but you weren't there. He hung around Conifer Lodge for a bit and when you didn't show up he returned to his flat.'

Valda had to bite her lips. She was tempted to tell the secretary/receptionist that she'd much rather hear all that from Adrian himself. Well, she thought scornfully, there was one person anyway who would be pleased that Adrian was going to be set free.

'Perhaps you'd tell Adrian that I shall be on duty again at four-thirty until nine.'

'Will you be going for your usual run?'

Valda replaced the receiver almost surreptitiously. How dare Merle Decarta presume so much! It made her sick—did Adrian tell *her* everything!

She gave vent to her anger by putting her bright blue

track suit on over shorts and tee-shirt and driving to the nearby school. It was the summer term now and the fund-raising events had been organised to coincide with school holidays so that the playing fields, gym and running track were available for use provided permission was requested of the caretaker.

Valda exchanged a few brief words with the caretaker's wife before going on to the track. As she passed the gym she could hear the hollow sounds of someone doing something there. She noticed several cars, one of which belonged to Sebastian, so Valda just prayed that he wouldn't come over to the track.

As she undid the zip of her track suit top she realised that it was slacker than a few weeks ago when she'd fetched it from Maple Cottage. She'd evidently lost a fair bit of weight since exercising and running regularly.

She did a few limbering-up exercises and then set off. Speed wasn't important, but the number of laps she could do. Some of her patients had sponsored her at ten and five pence per lap despite her protests. She assured them she didn't expect to be able to manage any more than ten at the most but as time and practice progressed she was running ten laps with ease. Today as she recalled her conversation with Merle Decarta she just kept running, hating the secretary/receptionist a little more with each few metres. She even lost count of her laps but eventually half-way round the track she began to feel her legs giving. She must get back to the car so she urged herself on until she was within a few feet of it, and then she slowed down, stopping at last to double up to breathe more easily.

Her ears were drumming, she imagined someone was clapping and then an arm went across her back, a hand searched for and pulled out the elasticated waist of her shorts.

'Clever girl,' Sebastian complimented, 'that was about fourteen laps.'

Valda managed to laugh as she tried to move out of

his grasp. 'Only because I was angry,' she said. 'Don't expect that kind of performance on the day.'

She went to her car and leaned over the bonnet, still panting.

'I shall expect even better and I'll find a way of making you mad on the day if that's what makes you keep going.'

Valda shook her head. Why didn't he just go away? He had hardly bothered to communicate with her of late apart from the usual polite conversation a consultant makes to his ward Sister when he's visiting patients.

She opened the passenger door of her car and sat sideways so that she could pull on her trousers.

'Haven't you got a towel? You know you should have a rub down.'

She reached over to the back seat and dried off the top half of her body with the small towel she'd brought. She knew he was watching every movement she made and she was embarrassed at the way her damp tee-shirt clung to her breasts.

'You've been overdoing it,' he said authoritatively. 'How many pounds have you lost?'

Valda shrugged. 'No idea,' she mumbled into the towel.

Sebastian snatched it from her. 'Then you should have. You don't seem to have any sense of responsibility.'

'Oh, for goodness' sake shut up,' Valda said crossly. 'You nag me into taking part, and now you're not blasted well satisfied!'

'I won't be if you're only a shadow of your former self when you walk up the aisle,' he said, and when she glared at him with contempt she detected a hint of pathos in his expression.

'That's my worry, not yours,' she stated firmly.

For once he didn't continue the argument. He couldn't be lost for words, not beaten, not the great crusading consultant!

She stood up to pull her track suit over her head and when she had zipped it up she glanced his way again petulantly.

The look was still there. His eyes were like gilded jewels and she quickly stuffed her hands into her pockets in an effort to forget the ring on her finger. She had no right to be wearing it, but it was valuable so she dared not leave it anywhere and she couldn't run with it swinging on a chain round her neck.

His tantalising eyes would always be her undoing. He mesmerised her and they stood confronting one another for several seconds before Valda could stand it no longer. She turned to go round the front of the car to get in the driver's seat.

'Now that you're so fit,' Sebastian said coolly, coming to rest his elbows on the passenger side and still abashing her with his stare, 'it's time you practised on the assault course. I'll expect you there this weekend.'

'You'll be lucky,' Valda tossed back and slammed shut her door, fastened her seat belt and started off, taking it for granted that he would move away.

She reached the school driveway aware that she wasn't dragging a body along, and she returned to Conifer Lodge where she showered and prepared to return to duty. She sat on the side of her bed and took a long hard look at her ring. If it was hers to keep for always it would have been an everlasting reminder of the man she loved no matter where fate took her in the future. But the very fact that she was bent on returning it to Adrian helped her for the moment to store away the passion she felt for Sebastian, and to contemplate what she was going to say to her fiancé. She mentally rehearsed many times words which were truthful, not too revealing and as kind as the situation would allow, but she knew that for all the rehearsing the words would tumble out of her mouth in a hopeless jumble when the time came.

There were lapses when she felt that her courage

would fail her. Impulsive moments of regret when she'd decide to let things ride along a natural course. In any event Adrian didn't seem to be in a hurry to see her and it was two days later before she found him propped up against the telephone kiosk outside the Jester inn when she'd been out running.

'Adrian!' she said in surprise, 'why didn't you phone? I didn't need to run today.'

'Mustn't stop the energetic,' he said sarcastically as he pecked her cheek.

'Didn't Merle give you my message?' Valda asked, still a little breathless. She sensed that Adrian was not overjoyed to see her. It was as if he was here by duty only.

'Yes, which was kind of her considering you hung up on her.'

Valda was surprised that Merle had mentioned this to Adrian.

'I was a bit annoyed to hear from her that you'd got back on Sunday night after all.'

'I was more than a little annoyed to discover you'd gone off in my absence,' Adrian countered stuffily.

'I went home for the weekend, but as Dad was taking Lee to Bristol to see his mother I went to Mary Kepple's to tea—that's all.'

'I hung around until ten o'clock. I was tired after the course and the journey,' he said as if she should have known that.

'But I wasn't expecting you back until Monday,' Valda insisted.

'My parents were away on holiday—abroad, of course.' There was bitterness in his voice. 'And I don't find my brothers and their families conducive to spending a whole weekend with. Come on, let's go and have a drink.'

'No, Adrian,' Valda said quickly before she weakened. 'Not tonight. I want to talk to you and it might be better out here.'

'You shouldn't stand around, you've been running, you'll get chilled.'

'Then walk me back to Conifer Lodge,' she suggested. 'I . . . I don't really know how to begin, but I honestly feel we've been a bit—well—hasty?' she began.

Adrian stopped walking. 'What do you mean?' he demanded.

'You swept me off my feet—I didn't stop to think,' she said softly.

'You mean one little tiff and we're finished?'

'No, Adrian, it's got nothing to do with that. I'm so very fond of you, but I think we've made a mistake.'

He swung her round in the lane and peered into her face. Valda could hear her heart drumming loudly. She supposed she'd done it all wrong, but now that she'd started she had to go through with it. Perhaps it would have been easier over a drink after all.

'So Merle was right,' Adrian said disdainfully.

That was sufficient to make Valda bristle with effrontery. 'Merle again?' she said sarcastically.

'It's Sebastian Carr, isn't it? The great man whom you always manage to sound so disparaging about. Merle said if I didn't hurry up he'd carry you off on a different sort of crusade while I was still trying to pluck up courage to pop the question. I suppose I was even too late when I did—sweep you off your feet?'

'Tell that Merle to mind her own business and not to judge other people by her own moral or immoral standards,' Valda exploded hotly. 'Sebastian Carr wouldn't waste his time on me when he's got the gorgeous Miranda and a house half built, now would he? So much for all the perfect Miss Decarta knows.'

'So why then?' Adrian asked calmly, appearing to have run out of steam.

'Because I would be cheating you, Adrian. If I'm really honest with myself I know that I don't feel—' she shrugged as she searched for words which had the right meaning without hurting him further, 'the right sort of

feeling that marriages are made of. I am fond of you,'
she repeated. 'It was a wonderful weekend and we've
had some good times, but it's better to make the break
now than to drift into a relationship full of platitudes.'

She reached round her neck and undid the chain.
Already Adrian's hand was held open to take the ring.

'I . . . I hope we can be friends just as we've always
been, Adrian?'

'Have your cake and eat it you mean?' he jibed.

'No, I didn't mean that—if I know what you mean
by that. I mean what I say, that I hope we shall remain
like mature sensible people on speaking terms.'

'Of course—only every time I meet Mr bloody-Carr
I shall feel like tying his tie a great deal tighter for him.'

'Don't say things like that, Adrian. It isn't you,'
Valda said, vexed.

'How do you expect a man to feel when he's just
been jilted for another man? Whatever you say, Valda,
I'm sure it's his influence—there's been something
between you from the moment you met.'

Valda walked on unable to repudiate what Adrian
was saying. He drew alongside her, placed his arm
round her shoulders as he said: 'I'm sorry. It would be
even worse to be jilted for no apparent reason. I'm only
sorry for you that Sebastian isn't free. Merle felt sure—'

'And I felt sure that you were falling for Merle,'
Valda cut in sharply.

Adrian laughed. 'The super-efficient daddy's darling,
Merle? She's good company I suppose, but she doesn't
turn me on. She'd have liked to be in the running for
Sebastian, but from what I can gather there's not a
woman in Addlefield who wouldn't like to be in that
position. So it's the delectable Miranda, is it? She's so
young, so—mm—' He let out a long, soft sigh and
Valda knew that she had never been exclusively his.

In the driveway of Conifer Lodge they parted with a
passive kiss, and Adrian made some pointless remark

about Valda's father having won after all.

She got to her room, relieved, yet sad that it was all, all over.

CHAPTER ELEVEN

VALDA paced her room for a while. She felt drained of all emotion except a yawning emptiness. She had done what she believed to be right, conscious of the pain she was causing Adrian, yet after the initial insult he'd taken it all matter-of-factly. She would miss him terribly, miss the nice little things about him, the frivolous things, the secrets they had shared, and somehow she suddenly felt much older. Was she wiser too? Was it wise to care for someone so much that anyone with an observant eye could see? It was going to be a traumatic time now while the grapevine spread the news of her broken engagement. She wasn't going to spread it. The know-all Merle could take care of that, but each day passed and no one mentioned anything to her. Was everyone being discreet or had Adrian decided to let her be the one to make it known? The longer it took the easier it would be, she hoped.

All her energies went into the coming sporting events. She watched the marker on the appeal thermometer rise rapidly. It was amazing how the money poured in, and how both sides of her sponsorship form quickly filled, and she was determined to make twelve laps on the running track if she could. She couldn't imagine what other events Sebastian had lined up for her, but as the days passed and he volunteered no further information she guessed that he had merely been teasing her.

Saturday came and she had a half-day off to be followed by late shift on Sunday. She'd trained hard so intended to let up a bit and rest during her off duty. Somehow she had to face her father, and she decided to save this up for the evening and then she could stay overnight at Maple Cottage.

After lunch she had a long rest on her bed, even managing an hour's sound sleep, and then with just a towel round her she went along the corridor to shower.

Two of her colleagues, dressed to go out, were coming along towards her. They were both girls she had trained with and they smiled and separated to pass her, but to her amazement they linked arms with her so that the towel slid to her feet and midst raucous laughter they almost carried her to the swing doors, threatening to take her to the floor below where some male nurses were holding a party. They would have done too, but their frivolity ended abruptly as one of them said, 'My God—a man!' They let Valda go and she slipped to the floor but as she heard the swing doors close she got up and through the glass saw the figure of a man talking to the girls, his hand already pushing the doors open again. Valda flung open the nearest door and dashed into the room of another of her colleagues who was resting on the bed.

'Do come in, don't bother to knock,' the girl said, then seeing that Valda was naked she sat up, letting her book fall to the floor. 'What on earth . . .?'

'Ssh!' Valda said, listening at the door. 'I think he's gone—some chap looking for someone and just when those clowns, Sharon and Kay, were acting the fool. Audrey—do me a favour and get my towel?' she implored. 'I'll have to go back to my room and get my sponge bag which I'd forgotten anyway. I was still half-asleep.'

Audrey raised her eyebrows and tut-tutted. 'That'll teach you to go around without your housecoat on. Nobody's safe and nothing's sacred in this place.'

She was only wearing bra and pants herself but she peeped outside and then ran along to retrieve Valda's towel.

'Could you spare it?' she asked, holding it up.

'I know, it's not the largest but it'll do. I must get

my towelling tabard when I get to my room. Thanks, you're a pal.'

'Any time—wish my book was as exciting as the things that go on here. You be careful now, I expect that chap is waiting to pounce on you in the shower.'

Valda left Audrey to her own witticisms. She opened her own door and let it shut loudly, but as she turned to take her tabard off the hook on the back of the door she drew in her breath and held it. Sebastian was sprawled across her bed.

'What are you doing here?' she breathed eventually. 'You'll get me the sack!'

He put two fingers on his lips. His eyes were overflowing with wickedness.

'Not if you keep quiet,' he said. Valda knew that the walls were paper-thin and if the occupant on either side of her room heard a man's voice all hell would break out. 'Hurry up—we're going to the Army base,' he informed her.

'It's my afternoon off and I'm having a break,' she said as adamantly as she could without raising her voice. 'I'm going to have a shower and you'd better be gone when I get back.'

For the second time in ten minutes she found herself towel-less. He held her slim waist and looked deep into her scared blue eyes. 'If I do what I want to do, my darling Nordic beauty, we'll still be here this time tomorrow. Now, on with your track suit and hurry.'

'No—damn you,' she said, pushing to keep him at arm's length. 'You don't dictate to me!'

He threw her down on the bed and although she struggled furiously he managed to get her briefs over her feet. She didn't have time to feel embarrassed as he tugged her tee-shirt over her head. She just couldn't fight lying back on the bed in such an awkward position so before she could even scream he had managed to make her presentable, and to make matters worse he was grinning triumphantly.

He bent over her and whispered: 'Now put your track suit on, gather up a dress and whatever else you need and if you're not out in ten minutes I'll be back.'

'Somebody will see you going out,' she said, her turn to gloat.

'No, darling—you're going to look out of the doorway to see that it's all clear. There's a party going on downstairs to which I was invited. I looked in so no one will be the least bit suspicious if I just walk out again. Now—move!' He pulled her up and she opened the door softly. Everywhere was quiet and when she motioned to him to go he went, patting her bottom as he did so.

Her hair looked bedraggled and she felt a mess, but she knew he'd have no hesitation in returning if she didn't do as he commanded. As she hastily put a lightweight dress in a bag with sandals and a cardigan she wondered if at last Merle had set the wheels of gossip in motion. Sebastian had only come for her because he felt sorry for her. Well, she'd soon put him right about that!

There was plenty of noise coming from a room on the ground floor so no one heard or noticed Valda go out through the conservatory to the car waiting by the kerb.

Sebastian leaned over and opened the door, but Valda ignored his provocative smile. She fastened the seat belt saying, 'Why do I just do what you say? I don't want to go on an assault course. That's a man's sport, and why can't I use my own car?'

He patted her knee. 'Just sit there and fume, or relax—whichever you prefer,' he said dispassionately.

She did fume too. Whenever he spoke she replied curtly and haughtily. What was he playing at?

It took three quarters of an hour to reach the Army camp and it was obvious that Sebastian was expected. A sergeant greeted them and a dishy young instructor took charge of Valda, taking her through each individual

obstacle. It was like nothing she had ever done before
and several times she suggested that she simply wasn't
fit enough, but the instructor took little notice of
anything she said, and she was pulled through pipes,
hauled over vaulting horses, water jumps and finally
shouted at to climb the rope ladder.

When she was totally exhausted she was given the
opportunity to rest. She looked round for Sebastian,
swearing vengeance on him, but he was fully occupied
with a group of officers. The instructor seemed amused
at her objections to taking part.

'You're a brave young lady,' he said, 'taking on three
doctors from the hospital on the day.'

'You may not believe this,' Valda said, 'but I haven't
volunteered to do any such thing, and that wretched
man over there is in for a shock because no way am I
going to be made to look a fool.'

'Oh, you won't look a fool, Valda. You're good and
I'd say in pretty good form, and from what I've seen of
some of the doctors you'll beat them hollow. Anyway,
if you're being sponsored it's finishing the course which
counts. Winning is a matter of personal achieve-
ment—or pride.' He turned and cast a glance towards
Sebastian. 'At least give him a run for his money.'

'You need loads of practice and there isn't enough
time. The events all take place next weekend. I shan't
waste your time again, don't worry.'

'I shall worry if you don't. Come on, where's your
sporting spirit?'

'She hasn't got any of that,' Sebastian said, joining
them, 'only intense hatred for me and the things I make
her do which is why she'll do it to give vent to her
spite.'

'Okay then,' the instructor said, 'let battle commence.
Valda, you have thirty seconds start.'

'No,' Valda said stubbornly. 'I didn't agree to this.'

But her protestations fell on deaf ears as Sebastian
held her hand and raced her to the first obstacle. He

gave her a sharp slap which sent her off in a fit of rage.

At each point there were soldiers hurling abuse at her to spur her on. She'd show Sebastian Carr a thing or two, but she was vaguely aware of him overtaking her at the wall. Her mind seemed to have gone numb. She ought to have stuck her ground she thought savagely as agony and pain racked her body. She leapt up on to the rope ladder with the instructor yelling at her from below, and then she was helped on to the platform and was soon swinging down to the ground once more.

Sebastian caught her and unleashed her.

'You beast—you absolute *pig*,' she yelled at him, beating his chest with her fists, and then with no breath left she slithered to the muddy grass and pummelled the ground, splattering her face with dirt.

The men were all laughing as Sebastian helped her up.

'I can see you're going to walk away with the prize,' Sebastian said. 'I shall have to put in more practice.'

The officers took them into the Mess for a cup of tea. Valda vowed that that was the end for her, but a sponsorship form with her name on it was full up with the names of the soliders and officers who had watched and were now admiring her performance.

Sebastian just went on grinning, even when they got back in his car and were returning to Addlefield.

'You could have dropped me off at Maple Cottage,' Valda said at length when she realised they were in the Deasley vicinity.

Sebastian didn't answer but sped on towards Addlefield, his face now set hard in grim determination.

He pulled in to the driveway of a large Victorian house set in its own grounds. By the little name cards at the front door Valda realised it was flats—one was his flat, she supposed, as she obstinately refused to get out of the car. She hardly had the strength to anyway.

'Darling, don't be so pig-headed. The least I can do

is to feed you and offer you a clean-up after all that exertion.'

She didn't seem to have the will-power to resist him so she followed him in and up to the first floor. The rooms were large, the ceilings high and it was all beautifully decorated and furnished.

He opened a door off of a landing.

'Shower? Or would you rather relax in the bath?' he asked.

'Bath, please,' she said dully. 'I haven't brought my toilet things or bath cap.'

'You'll find all you need in there. I have a shower cubicle in my room so take as long as you like. I can be preparing supper.'

The bathroom was spacious, tiled and fitted out in beige and dark brown with a few splashes of turquoise green to liven it up. Valda found the warm, oiled water soothing to her aching limbs and she was in danger of falling asleep when Sebastian called that the meal was almost ready.

She hadn't prepared for being entertained and now she realised how scantily clad she was going to be in the midnight blue crêpe dress which left her shoulders bare. It was held up by thin double straps, the bodice tight-fitting and the skirt flared. She was glowing too well to need her cardigan so she carried it over her arm and put her muddied track suit and other clothes into the bag.

She crossed the landing to the lounge. A table was set for a candlelit dinner. She hardly dared look to see whether it was for two or three, so she went to the television to look enviously at a large photograph of Miranda which was standing on the top.

Sebastian came up behind Valda and laughed. 'She's adorable, isn't she?' he crooned. 'My crazy, mixed-up niece who prefers her uncle's company to boy-friends.' He picked the photograph up and it was Miranda who was mocking Valda now.

Valda didn't believe she had heard aright but she didn't give Sebastian the pleasure of hearing her question it. Instead she heard herself saying, 'Maybe she's been let down at some time. She'll get over it—she's too pretty not to attract some nice man in the future.'

Sebastian replaced the photo and drew Valda to the table. He inclined his head and pursed his lips as if wondering whether or not to say what was on his mind.

'I rather think she's going to be grateful to you, my dear,' he said slowly.

'Me?' Valda echoed stupidly.

She's hoping she can catch Adrian on the rebound.'

Valda's head was in a whirl. Of course, she had nothing to fear from Miranda now—and Miranda was attracted to Adrian! Yes, that would be a good match, but where did Sebastian fit in? It didn't alter the fact that he was having a house built for his bride. Could it be Merle?

When Sebastian served huge steaks Valda managed to surface enough to realise that this was dinner for two.

'You know you shouldn't have,' she began as he helped her to green beans, peas and carrots.

'Got to keep your strength up, Valda. We can't have you pining away. I can't honestly say I'm sorry about you and Adrian, but if you're still in shock and there's anything I can do you only have to say,' and by the tone of his voice Valda knew he meant it.

She watched him as he lit the candles, then asked, 'How did you know my engagement was broken?'

'Merle told Miranda, Miranda rang me joyfully to tell me the news. You've made one young lady very happy,' he said.

Valda started to eat. What else had Adrian fed into the 'Merle' computer? she wondered, but Sebastian did not let her dwell on her own thoughts. He kept up a non-stop conversation throughout the meal, and as the minutes ticked away and the first course was followed by strawberries and cream and then coffee, she found herself talking to him just as if there had never been any animosity between them.

They washed up in harmony and returning to the lounge Sebastian asked, 'Am I forgiven?'

'For what?'

'Making you work like hell today to stimulate that intense sexual drive we talked about.'

Valda blushed furiously. '*You* talked about,' she said. 'I shall be darned glad when this crusade is all over.'

He placed his hands round her waist and drew her towards him. 'Darling, I have another one just beginning.'

She tried to prevent their bodies making contact. 'Oh, no,' she groaned, 'you can count me out.'

'I don't think so. This one involves just two people—you and me.'

She melted into his arms as he kissed her forcibly. She felt his fingers tangling in her hair, removing the pins to allow the silky tresses to fall free. Then he lifted handfuls of her hair and pulled her head forward. She hardly felt him unzip her dress but as she tossed her hair back she knew he was sliding the straps off her shoulders, and when her dress slipped away he covered her breasts with her hair.

'This is one crusade that I've won before you knew it had begun, darling,' he whispered, discarding her dress, and his powerful kiss drained her of all resistance. She'd admired his honey-dewed eyes, the curve of his tempting lips and now they moulded together eagerly, content to sink to the floor where the softness of the lambswool rug tickled her back and she arched herself towards him. Could what she really wanted be within her grasp?

He lifted her head and fanned her hair out on the rug above her, then paused looking down at her with longing in his wistful eyes. He ran a hand down her leg, tickled the soles of her feet so that she cried out and drew her legs up, then his fingers travelled up the back of her leg as he relished every inch of her.

'I could eat you,' he whispered. 'I should have saved the strawberries and cream as a dressing.'

Valda laughed. 'It might spoil the rug,' she giggled as she unbuttoned his shirt. He helped her and shrugged it off.

'No,' he said, 'I'd put it on all the exciting places and devour it before you could count to three.'

Later, as they still lay in each other's arms on the rug Sebastian said: 'You'll have to stay the night. This crusade is only to stimulate you to do well for me in the other one, and that means seven days of torture in between.'

'You're devious,' she told him, her fingers revelling in the feel of his virile body.

'One crusade leads to another, my darling, and I always see to it that each one is better than the last. Each one more exciting . . .'

Valda closed her eyes as his lips provocatively nibbled at hers, and his thumb kept up a stimulating rhythm over her hard nipple. Her body was instantly alive to the passion they shared. If this was crusading she liked it—she liked it a lot.

CHAPTER TWELVE

IN the cold light of day Valda despised herself for allowing him to persuade her to participate in his passionate crusade. He hadn't mentioned love, but taken advantage of the fact that her heart was brimming over with it. She should have known he was only playing with her emotions in order to get her to enter into every phase of his fund-raising efforts. There was no way out short of injuring herself, and she wouldn't want that and have to endure his wrath for he would be bound to think she had done it on purpose. So, during the week that followed she went out jogging at every opportunity and even went to the Army base on two evenings to get more practice in on the assault course. It was tough going and she had no doubt at all that she'd get the booby prize for that event. Each day when she went off duty she longed to be able to relax, but she didn't dare. Every joint and muscle protested at the cruel treatment she was giving her body, but she was determined to give as good an account of herself as she could, especially as her father and Mary would be there to urge her on, as well as many of the ex-patients who had sponsored her.

After Sebastian had done his round one morning he stopped for coffee.

'How's the training going then?' he asked.

Valda looked up at him hesitantly. She was finding it more and more difficult to look at him for fear of giving away too much of her thoughts. He hadn't mentioned anything about the effects their night of love had had on him, nor did he enquire about her feelings. Typical of a man, she supposed. Well, maybe he was used to one night stands, but not Valda Bergman, and she didn't intend to be used again. She was committed to doing her best in the forthcoming events for the benefit of the hospital, after that—she couldn't visualise what might happen.

'I'm doing my best,' she replied quietly.

'That's all I can ask of anyone, my dear Valda. You don't need to look so worried. Provided you get plenty of sleep, eat sensibly and with the minimum of practice I'm sure you'll easily finish your course and achieve your targets. All we want is some good weather, we certainly have the right attitude and winning spirit among all the competitors. I shall be in theatre tomorrow as usual and when I do my next round there are one or two who can be discharged in readiness for the new intake. There are about five children coming in; I hope you don't mind, but I much prefer to treat the children of school age during the school holidays—hope they won't cause too much havoc for you and your staff?'

Valda made a face. 'We'll try to cope,' she said.

'Good girl,' he returned, and with a pat on her back was gone.

Hm, she thought, the other night might never have happened. What was she to think?

But there wasn't too much time to think of anything but work, and if she wanted to forget the forthcoming weekend she wasn't allowed to as the staff were all so keen, and expected her to share in their eagerness.

Valda had to admit that the whole programme had been very well organised. Whether this was due to Sebastian's experience in such matters or whether Merle was responsible she didn't know, but the assault course was scheduled for the Friday evening so that she and others would benefit from a good night's sleep before having to do the five-mile race which started and ended at the hospital the following day. Those who could swim were going to take part as and when they were off duty during Saturday morning, while those taking part in the run would all need Saturday afternoon free. Arranging off duty was something of a headache as almost everyone was involved in one event or another or even all of them, and Valda was rather pleased that the assault course and the running events were her only involvement. She had to admire the junior nurses who were full of enthusiasm.

Sebastian was surprised and somewhat irritated to find her on duty on Friday afternoon. 'Should you be here?' he asked curtly.

'I do work here, Mr Carr,' she retorted.

'And you've quite a task ahead of you this evening. Rest and practice in equal amounts should have been the order of the day, I would have thought.'

'Work keeps me fit. I was off duty this morning, and this evening I can only do my best. You got me into the assault course so don't blame me if I let you down.'

'You'll not only be letting me down, but yourself and the people who have sponsored you. I'm surprised at your attitude this late in the day—still, maybe it's last minute nerves.' He seemed to be eyeing her suspiciously.

'My attitude hasn't changed since you first approached me,' she said with feeling. 'I hate having to ask people for money. It's as simple as that.'

'No one is asking anyone for their last penny, and who knows even you may one day benefit from an eye specialist and his modern ideas.'

'I do appreciate the need for the latest equipment,' she said heatedly, 'but I believe I made it quite plain at the beginning that I object to being pressurised.'

'And I repeat that I know you like being dominated, and now that Adrian is no longer your master someone has to take you in hand.'

'You really are insufferable,' she snapped angrily. 'I can well do without your interference. 'You've involved me in the assault course which I didn't want to do, I'm running in the five-mile race, I'll do the track run in a week's time and that is *all* .'

'Have I asked for any more? I suppose you'd like me to get down on bended knee and beg?' He leaned over her and grinned wickedly. 'I will have you begging, Valda, sooner than you think—for mercy. Now, would you like me to pick you up and take you to the Army base, or are you going to continue being stubborn? Don't forget you might not be in a fit state to drive by the time we've finished.

'I shall be quite as capable as you, and I'd rather travel alone, thank you.' she said by way of dismissal. His bleeper went then so he turned and stalked away.

Valda didn't know how she got through that afternoon. She despised Sebastian Carr for getting her into tricky situations and she was far from happy about the forthcoming assault course. She would be thankful when it was all over.

Everyone wished her well when she went off duty, their confidence in her making her feel even more inadequate. She made time for a honey sandwich and a cup of tea before changing into her track suit and setting out.

When she drove into the car-park at the base she was surprised to see that quite a crowd had gathered. Not many females had entered so one girl was competing against three males in each heat. Valda found to her dismay that she was up against Sebastian, Duncan Fraser, who was known to be a great athlete, and Ray Pyke who was a reasonable all-rounder.

'Glad to see you didn't chicken out,' the Army sergeant greeted with a warm smile. 'If we'd put all you girls together I have no doubt that you'd have won by a sizeable margin, but with the Scotsman none of you stand a chance.'

'Oh, thanks very much,' Valda laughed. 'Makes me wonder why I *didn't* chicken out.'

'Because you're going to give your boss the hell of a run for his money and I'll be behind you all the way. I believe the more I abuse you the better you'll do.'

'Hm, men! You do get some funny ideas.'

'That's why you can't do without us. You beat your boss and I'll take you out to dinner.'

'You're on,' Valda said, knowing full well that she didn't have a chance, and the sergeant's money was safe enough.

The waiting seemed endless, they limbered up while the contestants gathered and at last the first four were off, and as each subsequent heat took place the shouts grew wilder.

All Valda wanted was for her heat to be over and done with. The previous heat delayed things as one of the contestants broke his ankle jumping off the wall, but at last she was on her marks and sent off with thirty seconds start. She closed her mind to everything except the sergeant yelling in her ears, and she couldn't believe it when she went into the tunnel that so far she was unaware of anyone in close proximity. She even scaled the rope ladder without mishap, but when she took the water jump she felt the presence of a man on either side and then she knew she was doomed. The sergeant shouted louder, the crowd roared their encouragement and Valda just set her sights on the wall. Breathless, she hung on for dear life as she swung to the ground at the same time as one of the other contestants and then it was a race under the net to the finishing line. Sebastian beat her by a mere whisker, but they were both beaten by the tough Scotsman, Duncan Fraser, and Ray Pyke came in a close fourth.

Valda bent forward, gasping for air. She felt an arm round her and as she straightened up Sebastian kissed her, much to the delight of the spectators.

When she could finally get her breath back she said: 'Don't know what that's for.'

'I'm proud of you, Valda. Three men were tough opponents but you finished the course and did exceptionally well. Congratulations.'

Duncan came up then and congratulations were

exchanged all round, and only then did Valda realise that the crowd were shouting for an encore.

'Good heavens,' she said, 'what do they want, blood?'

'No, darling, I fancy they want this.' Sebastian enclosed her in his arms and kissed her passionately for all the world to see. Valda tried to fight him off but she could only go limp in his arms as he took her last breath away.

The sergeant came up to Valda as Sebastian let her go. 'That was splendid, Valda, and the dinner date still stands.'

'I don't deserve it but it's a lovely invitation.'

'We'll be at the grand finale when all the events are finished in a week's time so I'll see you then, if not before.'

He turned and went back to organise the following heats and at the end of the day it was Duncan who came out the winner, but as the sergeant announced it was finishing the course that really mattered and everyone had achieved that, except the unfortunate two who had sustained minor injury.

Valda regained her breath and felt reasonably pleased and thankful that it was all over. She went across to where her father and Mary Kepple were waving frantically. 'My dear, you were very brave,' Mary said, giving Valda a kiss.

'I suppose it wasn't too awful, though I expect 'sir' expected me to do better, but at least he only just beat me.'

'Nonsense, Nordic beauty, I let you nearly beat me,' Sebastian teased, coming up and standing with his arm firmly round her waist. 'We'll expect better things tomorrow afternoon, won't we, Howard?'

'She'll do her best, and she was quite hard to beat in the old days, eh, Valda?'

'That was a long time ago, Dad, but I do enjoy running and it's good to be active again. It was nice of you to come. What have you decided to go for tomorrow? There's so much on—the swimming, the race, the church fête and jumble-sale?'

'I had thought about offering my services in the football match, but I don't think they'd have me,' her father said.

'It's your money Mr Carr wants,' Valda quipped.

'Your father has not only sponsored you, young lady, but I hope you've sponsored him in the darts match next week.'

'I haven't, but I will. Looks as if I shall have to take out a mortgage to settle my debts,' Valda laughed.

'It's all in an excellent cause,' Mary said.

'They're serving refreshments over there,' Sebastian explained and they made their way over to the kiosk being run by the Army caterers.

Sebastian was called away then and from the crowd Adrian and Miranda emerged. Valda didn't feel the slightest bit awkward as they congratulated her on her performance. They chatted for a while and then Valda said her goodbyes and went back to Conifer Lodge.

She was glad that things had turned out well for Adrian and Miranda, she only wished that she knew what course her future was going to take.

Sebastian was very fond of making her a public example, he loved to tease, but didn't he realise just how crazy she was over him?

The next morning Valda woke to find that it had rained quite heavily overnight. It was an overcast, sticky kind of day and not ideal for running, especially a five-mile race, but by midday the sky had lightened a little and after her four hours on duty she prepared for the event which was to commence at the hospital car-park.

The starting gun was fired and the fifty strong line of contenders set off, some at a ridiculous pace which Valda knew from experience they would not be able to sustain, so she concentrated on her own pace and capability. The route took them through country lanes, skirting the town of Addlefield, along the river bank, across some fields and back to the hospital. By the time Valda reached the town there was a long line of single runners; she had no idea who was heading the race or how many had dropped out, she just kept going. Somewhere she supposed Sebastian was in the race but she tried not to think of him or the fact that he would most certainly be at the front. When they passed the Health Centre and Sports Club many people were lining the pavements to wave them on and Valda was aware of a cheer going up as she sped on. It was pleasantly cool by the river, though more difficult to run across the fields but now she knew that she was nearing the finishing line which she did with comparative ease, and was surprised to learn that she was first home.

She accepted a long cool drink and turned in time to see Sebastian come in with several others.

'You cheated,' he said. 'I lost sight of you so someone must have given you a lift en route.' But she knew he was joking and with a kiss he congratulated her. 'Becoming quite a habit,' he said softly, 'but one I could easily get addicted to.'

She wanted to tell him to go ahead, but instead she said, 'Is there any need to be quite so obvious? You'll have everyone talking.'

'You mean they aren't already?'

'I'm quite sure they are and I think I've provided enough fuel just lately.'

'Don't be such a spoilsport. They've got to talk about someone.'

Valda felt she would never get the better of him so she turned to see the other competitors come in. She had done her best and could now try to ignore him until next weekend when she was to take part in the track event. After that the fun would be all over she supposed and they could get back to a more normal way of life.

In the days that followed Sebastian was kept busy outside working hours with organising the remainder of

events and Valda kept up her training. The whole town
and village seemed to have been geared to involve
themselves in the fund-raising and it was soon announced
that more than the sum required had been raised. In
spite of her antagonism towards Sebastian and his
efforts she was delighted that it had all been successful.
It had even helped to brirg members of the hospital
staff much closer together whereas before the occasional
dance had been the only social event. When Valda next
looked at the notice-board she discovered that a grand
barbecue was to be held for everyone connected in any
way with the fund-raising. She learnt that the garden of
Conifer Lodge had been suggested but as this was rather
small a farmer nearby had allocated a field close to the
river, and the landlord of the Jester inn had offered to
undertake all the catering and drinks. Clearly it was
meant to be a grand finale and the staff were all very
excited.

Valda wasn't sure how she felt about it and decided
to wait until after the Saturday events had taken place.
The track event was now the only remaining one. She
arrived in good time and believed that she might manage
more than a dozen laps since doing so well in the five-
mile race. The school running track was the venue which
by now she was well used to. She did a few exercises
and ran a few paces before the start was officially
announced. This time the contestants were divided into
male and female so that only two runs were necessary
as the event had not been widely supported. The girls
had a good start and Valda was grateful for Pam
Gardner's help in lapping her. She just kept going and
only began to realise the lap number when it reached
ten. She began to feel her muscles pulling a little and
two laps later noticed that she was puffing a great deal.
Common sense told her that she had reached her peak
but she was determined to continue. After all the great
Mr Carr had sponsored her in this event and she meant
him to have to dig deep into his pocket. Three laps later

and she was decidedly uncomfortable and slowing considerably—just one more, she told herself, just one more—then suddenly her thigh muscle tightened, she stumbled, tried to keep her balance but the pain was excruciating and she was forced to go down and roll over in agony.

Valda didn't know much about the next few minutes. Two St John's Ambulance men who were on duty were quickly at her side to treat her and the pain lessened until she tried to stand up. She was forced to place an arm round each of the men and was more or less carried off the track. Tears of anguish and disappointment trickled down her cheeks as they helped her into the school where she was placed on a table and the hospital physiotherapist came to give her some massage. After a few minutes the door opened and Sebastian burst in. 'You little fool!' he admonished. 'Surely you've got enough common sense to know when your body has had enough.' Then seeing her tears he pushed aside the physiotherapist and took Valda in his arms. 'Oh, my silly darling, what were you trying to prove, for God's sake? It was supposed to be a fun run. Hospital staff are expected to know how to be sensible.'

'I meant to make you pay for all the nasty things you say and do,' she sobbed.

'Instead it's you who are paying for your pig-headedness. Thank goodness it's nothing serious, but you do realise that you're going to have to walk on it to exercise it. For now though we'll let you rest for a few hours. Come on, let me get you back to Conifer Lodge.'

Valda was quite content to be assisted in every way and the initial pain began to decrease gradually, though she was glad when she was left alone for a while. It was later in the day when someone brought her a tray of food and soon afterwards Sebastian called to see how she was feeling.

'You aren't allowed to just walk into the Sister's quarters whenever you feel like it,' she reproached in embarrassment. 'The pain has eased considerably so I can manage perfectly well now, thank you.'

'Good, then we can expect to see you at the barbecue this evening?'

'I don't think so, I'd rather just take things quietly for the rest of today.'

'What I have in mind is certainly nothing strenuous. I'll come for you at around eight o' clock—and no arguments!' he said, waving a warning finger at her.

She was feeling quite ashamed of herself for causing so much trouble, but staying in her room was boring to say the least, so she had a bath and dressed leisurely in a cotton trouser suit in a shade of bright tomato red which showed off her blonde hair admirably. At a few minutes to eight o' clock she went down to the sitting room in Conifer Lodge and almost at once Sebastian arrived. He smiled and with a cheeky wink said: 'Red, for danger? I see you managed the stairs all right without my help. Independent to a fault, or were you playing safe?'

'I'm sure I don't know what you're talking about, and I'm only coming because it's so boring in my room. I could have gone home, but no doubt Dad will be out with Mary Kepple.'

'Indeed he will, they'll be at the barbecue and he's very concerned about you, so let's get going.'

It was a perfect evening and the crowd that gathered in the field were in very good spirits. They met up with Valda's father and Mary, and Sebastian settled Valda in a garden chair while he went to fetch some food. There was plenty of wine too and Valda was pleased she had made the effort to come. Howard and Mary went home soon after the music was turned up and the disco began, and Sebastian and Valda walked them to the car to say their goodbyes.

'I doubt that dancing on an uneven surface will be good for you,' Sebastian said. 'So how about a walk by the river?'

Valda agreed and as darkness replaced the orange sun setting on the horizon he pulled her towards him in a passionate embrace.

'I think it's time to go back,' she said, trying to disentangle herself.

'Not until you've agreed to get involved in my next crusade.'

'Oh, no!' Valda groaned and tugged her arm free, but he was too quick for her and held her fast, kissing her firmly on her protesting mouth.

'This one will be much more demanding than anything you've ever got involved in before, my sweet. It means total surrender and a lifetime's commitment—I'm wholly averse to separation and divorce.'

'What on earth are you talking about?' Valda snapped irritably. 'From now on my time will be my own. You've got what you wanted and even you can't get blood out of a stone. People have had enough, Sebastian.'

'What I want now, *all* I want now, my darling, is a yes from you, a yes to the best crusade in the world. A crusade which will take us through future campaigns together as one. You can't be naïve enough not to understand what I'm saying? I love you, my Nordic beauty, and I know you love me, so—when, is all that's left to decide.'

Valda could hardly believe her ears and she fell against him with a sigh which told him what her answer was.

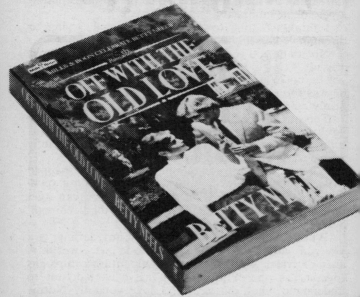

Doctor Nurse Romances

Romance in modern medical life

Read more about the lives and loves of doctors and nurses in the fascinatingly different backgrounds of contemporary medicine. These are the three Doctor Nurse romances to look out for next month.

DOCTOR MALONE, I PRESUME?
Holly North

THE ULTIMATE CURE
Jennifer Eden

NURSE ON LOAN
Ann Jennings

Buy them from your usual paperback stockist, or write to: Mills & Boon Reader Service, P.O. Box 236, Thornton Rd, Croydon, Surrey CR9 3RU, England. Readers in Southern Africa — write to: Independent Book Services Pty, Postbag X3010, Randburg, 2125, S. Africa.

Mills & Boon
the rose of romance

YOU'RE INVITED TO ACCEPT
4 DOCTOR NURSE ROMANCES
AND A TOTE BAG

 FREE!

Doctor Nurse

Acceptance card

NO STAMP NEEDED	Post to: Reader Service, FREEPOST, P.O. Box 236, Croydon, Surrey. CR9 9EL

Please note readers in Southern Africa write to:
Independant Book Services P.T.Y., Postbag X3010, Randburg 2125, S. Africa

YES! Please send me 4 free Doctor Nurse Romances and my free tote bag – and reserve a Reader Service Subscription for me. If I decide to subscribe I shall receive 6 new Doctor Nurse Romances every other month as soon as they come off the presses for £6.60 together with a FREE newsletter including information on top authors and special offers, exclusively for Reader Service subscribers. There are no postage and packing charges, and I understand I may cancel or suspend my subscription at any time. If I decide not to subscribe I shall write to you within 10 days. Even if I decide not to subscribe the 4 free novels and the tote bag are mine to keep forever. I am over 18 years of age   EP23D

NAME _____
                                        (CAPITALS PLEASE)

ADDRESS _____

_____

_____ **POSTCODE** _____

The right is reserved to refuse application and change the terms of this offer. You may be mailed with other offers as a result of this application. Offer expires September 30th 1987 and is limited to one per household. Offer applies in UK and Eire only. Overseas send for details.

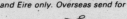